Allan McFadden trained as a secondary school music teacher, and has worked as teacher, actor, musician, music director and orchestrator. With fellow Australian, Peter Fleming, he has written several stage musicals: *Airheart*, *Madame de*, *Frank Christie*, *Frank Clarke* and *Noli me Tangere*. His first published novel is *Big Gig in Rock 'n' Roll Heaven*. *A Bientot, Mate!* is the second book in the Dougay Roberre series following on from *Au Revoir, Mate!* All three books are published by Austin Macauley Publishers.

For
Chris Blackam
who insisted on a second story

Allan McFadden

A BIENTOT, MATE!
(SEE YOU SOON, MATE!)

Book Two in the Dougay
Roberre Series

AUSTIN MACAULEY PUBLISHERS™
LONDON • CAMBRIDGE • NEW YORK • SHARJAH

Copyright © Allan McFadden 2023

The right of Allan McFadden to be identified as author of this work has been asserted by the author in accordance with sections 77 and 78 of the Copyright, Designs and Patents Act 1988.

All rights reserved. No part of this publication may be reproduced, stored in a retrieval system, or transmitted in any form or by any means, electronic, mechanical, photocopying, recording, or otherwise, without the prior permission of the publishers.

Any person who commits any unauthorised act in relation to this publication may be liable to criminal prosecution and civil claims for damages.

This is a work of fiction. Names, characters, businesses, places, events, locales, and incidents are either the products of the author's imagination or used in a fictitious manner. Any resemblance to actual persons, living or dead, or actual events is purely coincidental.

A CIP catalogue record for this title is available from the British Library.

ISBN 9781398471160 (Paperback)
ISBN 9781398471177 (ePub e-book)

www.austinmacauley.com

First Published 2023
Austin Macauley Publishers Ltd®
1 Canada Square
Canary Wharf
London
E14 5AA

Notes

All characters and situations in *A Bientot, Mate!* are fictional. They bear no resemblance to anyone alive or dead.

The areas and streets of Nice, Aubagne and Milan exist, though the buildings occupied by the characters do not.

A bientot (French) means 'see you soon'.

Au revoir (French) means 'farewell' or 'goodbye'.

Ca va? (French) means 'How's it going?' or 'How are you going?'

Maman (French) means 'mother'.

Un flic (French) means 'a cop'.

Oblozene chlebicky (Czech) is an open sandwich consisting of ham, onion and soft cheese.

Heidi, is a work of children's fiction, written by Swiss author Johanna Spyri. It was originally published in 1881 in two parts. *Heidi: Her Years of Wandering and Learning* and *Heidi: How She Used What She Learned.*

Joyeux Noel (French) means 'Merry Christmas'.

Bon soir, mes amis (French) means, 'good evening, my friends'.

Mate (Australian) is a term for a friend, though it can be used ironically.

Chapter 1

According to the calendar, autumn was sliding into winter. According to my feet, it had already slid there. I'm not a fan of winter. I know those snow-covered mountains, dominating Swiss postcards, look beautiful. However, that's how I like to view them – from afar. I do not like trudging through snow, slipping and sliding, three steps forward, one step back, trying desperately to stay upright, praying that at my destination there will be waiting for me a sensual snow bunny with a hot alcoholic reward. There never is. Winter can be so disappointing.

I was now beginning to sleep with a blanket beneath my Princess-Grace-rejected pink duvet with lace trim. That's who Remy, my friend who owns a warehouse of furniture and bric-a-brac, had told me owned it, when I asked of its origin, having stumbled upon it in amongst all his other suspiciously acquired goods.

For knock-a-bout wear, I'd replaced my quality leather jacket with a yellowy brown jacket made from goat's skin, lined with sheep's wool. I'd also found it in Remy's warehouse – in the section where he kept his 'best things'. I now regularly wore the scarf Madame Legrande had knitted for me at the end of the summer. She is a little old lady, who lives in the apartment on the ground floor, back towards the elevator. As I traipsed the streets, I looked like I should have been herding goats somewhere on a windswept hill, overlooking the Aegean to the east of here.

'Here' is Nice – affordable French city on the Cote d'Azur. I came to Nice from Sydney, Australia, nine months ago. I'd been taken there, at the age of three, by my French parents. They were whisked off from somewhere in France to the other side of the world and placed in a witness protection program. I had a great life out there – sun, sand, sustenance and sex. To be honest, I experienced a lot of the first three.

My name is Dougay Roberre – officially, Douglas Roberts – though I have no idea if that was the name I was baptised with. Probably not, as it doesn't sound terribly French, does it? I can't honestly say if I was ever baptised. I have no photographs of my parents, though I do know they loved me, never abused me, and taught me right from wrong. I do not need a photograph of them because their memory is burned so deeply and affectionately in my heart and mind, that I will never forget them. They died of natural causes back there in Sydney.

I speak excellent French, courtesy of them, though I can't read it, and I'm unable to write it. I'm not illiterate – I simply learnt all my reading and writing skills in English. As I approached my fortieth birthday, I had an overwhelming urge to return to the land of my birth; live, as in Sydney by the sea; and Nice was the only place I could afford along the French Riviera.

I sold my apartment overlooking Bondi Beach and bought one here – a converted double attic on top of a Belle Epoque building opposite Place Mozart, between the Gare de Nice and the Mediterranean, on Avenue Auber. Around me are streets named after famous composers – Rossini, Gounod and Saint-Saens. Occasionally a silly tourist will wander down one of the streets whistling or singing a tune composed by the street's name. On Rue Beethoven you can hear sung poorly the opening of his Fifth Symphony and around Place Mozart you hear a lot of, what Madame Legrande told me was titled, 'Eine Kleine Nachtmusik'.

After my short time here, I've managed to gather a few friends; two ex-lovers – one uninterested and the other living in New York; and an occasional enemy.

I do what I can to stay alive, taking on any form of employment which comes my way, within reason, as I do not possess one certificate of achievement recognised in any country in the world. Therefore, I'm a jack-of-all-trades, a man for hire.

To the French: *Je m'appelle Dougay Roberre, L'Homme Engager.*

Through the autumn, I've been working at *L'Opera Mozart*, a cafe near my apartment. During the summer that's just gone, the owner, Claude Tanguay, had given me intermittent shifts in his kitchen, which meant clearing away tables and washing up plates and cutlery. The best thing he did for me was to introduce me to his solicitor, Francine Delange, for whom I delivered documents. Some of the documents required a fist or two to enable a signature to be added by a reluctant 'client'. I also did other things for Francine, very enjoyable things, and she certainly returned the favour. She's the uninterested ex-lover.

At *L'Opera Mozart*, I was standing in for Claude's partner, both business and personal, Marcel Valiquette. He has an impressive name, though I don't think he is much of an impressive person. The times he'd served me as a customer, he was always surly, and after I subbed for him, he'd criticise my washing up skills and placement of cutlery. We'd never be friends. Whereas Claude, his older lover and brains in the operation, was an honest and friendly man, for whom I enjoyed working.

Claude, dressed in his usual black waistcoat over an ironed white shirt, walked into the kitchen as I was drying the last of the glasses.

"Ever think of getting in a chef?" I asked. "Expanding your business – offering sit-down meals?"

"Dougay, you are full of wild ideas. First, you recommend I play the music of Mozart, and now you want me to pay an enormous sum to a prima donna behind a frypan."

"The music has been a success. Besides, as I explained, the cafe is called…"

"Yes, yes, yes, to that – and no, no, no, to the idea of the chef. I can't afford it. And it's too much of a hassle."

"Claude," I paused for effect, for I was now serious. "That room back there, is it yours? Is it part of the cafe?"

"Yes," he admitted, suspiciously.

"What do you intend doing with it?"

He sighed and walked away.

I dried my hands and poured myself a large glass of water. As Claude turned out the last remaining light, I sat in the gloom, sipping it. Water – sometimes I live a wild and carefree existence. I took out my phone and hit the only piece of music I had on it – *I Get a Kick Out of You*. Sinatra sang to me.

The music link had been sent by Mary-Anne Walton. She's the ex-lover in New York. She's 'ex' because she's out of reach, not because we had an argument and she flew away. She was always planning on flying away – just not planning on getting involved with me over her last weekend in Cannes. I've often doubted since she's been gone, whether she'd really fallen for me or not. She still calls me and I still call her. I tell her I can't wait for the return of the sun and of her, as next season I have plans for a wonderful summer. The occasional bouts of insecurity in this long-distance relationship are all down to me.

Why? Well, Mary-Anne is gorgeous and I'm not. If I was gay, I'd be very uninterested in a man like me. To be honest, I do put myself down a bit, as I'm not all unappealing. I have been called 'slightly rugged-looking'. It was said to me, back in Sydney, by a woman I thought loved me. If I remember correctly, she said it with dripping irony, as she disappeared out of my life.

Also, what really worries me is that Mary-Anne and I have nothing in common, except a wonderful desire to jump each other's bones. She works in a world I'd never be involved in – film production – as a personal production assistant to international movie producer Harold Kempenski. At the moment she's supervising the post production (whatever that is) of Kempenski's latest film, *Au Revoir, Mate!*, the title of which came courtesy of me, and not the acclaimed Hollywood writer, Philip J. Phillips, who's credited with it.

It stars the late Calvin de Marko, and Mary-Anne feels that it's going to be a sensational hit, not only for the fact that it's a great story, and that Calvin's performance is wonderful, but also because Calvin died three days after shooting had wrapped. The publicity department, she told me, was now working overtime to draw the obvious parallels with James Dean. Mary-Anne said to me cynically, though truthfully, "Hollywood plus heart-throb plus tragedy equals gold."

I won't be mourning the loss of that murderous bastard, Calvin de Marko. In Los Angeles, I was told they'd held a drive-thru memorial service for him, covered on live television. Cars choked the streets. Here in Nice, less than ten of us attended the funeral for Danielle Hubert, the woman he'd choked.

The first time I met Danielle, she was bouncing off to swim in the sea, her blonde hair catching eyes, turning heads and breaking hearts. Now she would be forever swimming in the heavens and breaking the hearts of the angels up there.

I drained my water, left the cafe and walked home to bed. The building manager of my apartment block, the irrepressible M'sieur Pom, greeted me from behind his desk as I entered the foyer.

"What, no damsel in distress on your arm tonight?" he asked, cheekily.

"No. However if she should arrive a little later, send her up, please."

He laughed. Over the months I'd been living here, we had grown to appreciate each other's take on life and love and the foolishness attached to both.

I pulled open the elevator's cage and rode it up to a dinner of left over re-heated pasta, followed by an English language book in bed. Ah, the high life on the French Riviera!

*

The descending elevator stopped at the fourth floor. An elderly man climbed in, as I held open the iron door for him. He looked carefully at me. "Are you the Australian who lives in the attic?" he asked.

"Yes, monsieur. And you are?"

"Monsieur Degas."

"A famous name," I answered.

"Sadly, the talent did not blossom on our side of the family tree." He coughed, unhealthily.

Too many cigarettes as a young man, I assessed, though I did not offer him my 'doctor's opinion'. "Pleased to meet you, Monsieur Degas," I said, offering him my hand instead.

He took it. "It is a pleasure for me also, Monsieur Roberre." I guess by now everyone in the building knew who I was. On the ground floor I let him walk in front of me. He stopped to chat with M'sieur Pom.

A text message pinged on my mobile. It was from Francine Delange. She wanted me to deliver some papers which I knew would be waiting with her secretary. Since our breakup, the material was always waiting in the front office. However, this morning, the young secretary waved me through.

"Well, this is a pleasure," I said, walking by Francine, as she held the door for me.

"No need for sarcasm, Dougay," she said in that velvety voice I occasionally hear in my dreams.

"I meant it – honestly."

Francine Delange was still as gorgeous as she'd ever been, even if it had only been less than two months since I'd seen her. She was a couple of years older, however she didn't look it and I certainly didn't feel she was, when she had her arms around me, kissing me. Don't let me tell you how young she felt when she turned out the light!

Today she was in her familiar 'business is business' mode, not wasting any time coming to the point. "Remember Monsieur Lemoine?" she asked.

"Lemoine! How could I ever forget?" Delivering papers to be signed by Lemoine had been my first job for Francine. It had taken a fist or two to convince him to sign on the dotted line.

"Yes, a truly memorable person," she conceded, her tone dripping sarcasm. I'm sure she'd have loved to have said something else to describe the man, however ladies will be ladies.

"Oh, he's not that bad," I admitted. "It's the foul mouthed, blousy woman I've dubbed 'Lemoine's tart' who'll knife you in the leg." Francine gave me a curious look, not quite understanding or perhaps not quite wanting to know. "Another signature is required?" I asked, refocusing our meeting.

"Yes and no. I'd like you to hand this to him." She slid across the desk a similar looking envelope to the one I'd delivered that first time. Attached to it were three fifty-euro notes.

"Three?" I questioned, as last time she'd only paid me two.

"In case there's any trouble," she explained. I shrugged off her concern, thanked her, and folded them into my shirt's top pocket.

She went on to explain. "I need proof that he's received these documents. He can either sign the receipt inside – or you could take a photograph with your phone. He needs to be holding up the document to make sure the heading and date are clearly visible."

I thanked her again and left. I'd have loved to have lingered, however that was the reason we fell apart – my lingering outside her apartment block, drunkenly telling her via the intercom that I loved her, when all she wanted was a Friday night liaison.

I hadn't expected Lemoine to have changed address, so I went directly to his familiar front door. I knew he hadn't relocated, as the same junk outside it was in the same position as last time. I knocked.

"What the fuck do you want?" shouted Lemoine's tart, before she'd opened the door. When she did, she glanced up from the door clasp and caught my welcoming smile. She recognised me. "Fuck off! You – you…" She was lost for words – I have that effect on women! She thought about slamming the door, however she checked herself, looking down to see where my foot was placed. It was between the open door and the door jam, just like last time. She was a fast learner, for on my previous visit the door had rebounded and smacked her on the chest.

I pushed her out of the way.

"Fuck off!" she screamed.

"I see your love for the French language has not left you," I quipped.

I headed out the back to the kitchen where I expected to find Lemoine smoking a foul-smelling cigarette over a half empty cup of black coffee. He was. As a nod to the cooler weather, his dirty singlet was now covered by an open flannelette shirt.

"Hey! Lemoine!" I called breezily.

He looked up suddenly. "You!" he spat back in disgust.

"I need your signature on a receipt or a photograph of you receiving it – your choice. That's the kind of guy I am today – the client gets to choose," I added with a smile he didn't deserve.

"What the fuck is this?" he asked. I immediately had the distinct impression he was reluctant to accept the envelope.

"Weren't you listening?" He didn't answer. Rather he stood there belligerently stupefied. "Sign or pose!" I said harshly, reaching for my phone and tapping the camera icon.

"Are you going to hit me again?" he asked, concerned for his wellbeing.

"Only if you don't make a decision," I explained reasonably, man to man.

"Okay, okay – photograph." He limped to me. He hadn't fully recovered from the knife wound in his thigh, accidentally inflicted by the crazy woman he was living with, and who was still muttering obscenities at me from somewhere back down the hallway.

I took out the receipt. He held it beneath his chin. "Would you like me to smile?" he asked, sarcastically.

I appreciated his attitude. "If you weren't such a dead-shit, Lemoine, I reckon you'd be a reasonable guy to know." I hit the round red symbol, capturing his less than handsome features above the required receipt notice.

Lemoine's tart's scream suddenly exploded behind me. I jumped to the side as she lunged at me with her kitchen knife. I smacked her wrist. "Drop it!" I smacked it again with a savage chop which hurt me, as I'd hit her radius down near the wrist. As I rapidly shook my hand, trying to fling out the pain, her knife clattered onto the floor.

"But she," I hissed at Lemoine, "I can never be friends with." I raised my voice to the howling woman, "Turn around and put both your hands on that wall – up high!"

She stood her ground. "Make me," she said, as if she was a spoilt child playing a dare.

I hit Lemoine in the solar plexus with a left. He screamed and buckled over.

"Lemoine – tell her to do it, or I'll punch you again!"

"Do it!" he shouted at her, holding his guts. "Do what he says, you dumb stupid bitch."

"No one tells me what to do." She was digging in for the long haul.

I hit Lemoine again, though I pulled the punch. He screamed through expectation, rather than realisation.

"And don't call me stupid!" shouted the woman at Lemoine. "A bitch I might be, but I'm not fucking stupid!"

Lemoine's patience had now dissipated. He grabbed her and flung her against the wall. "Do it! Put your fuckin' hands on the wall. Neither of us wants to be stabbed!"

When she had finally calmed, with her raised arms and face to the wall, I headed to the front door.

"Hey!" Lemoine called after me. I turned as he hobbled my way. He dropped his voice and asked confidentially, "When are you going around to beat the shit out of her brother for assaulting you?"

I then knew that Lemoine and the woman had never made the connection. One night I'd been beaten up by two unknown assailants, who drove an old Renault. Lemoine's tart had set them onto me. I'd had my revenge on her brother and his mate by sticking a toothpick in each valve of their car's tyres.

"I like the element of surprise. They can wait," I lied.

He limped closer in to me. "I can't wait for her brother to get a good smacking! He dislikes me intensely – thinks I'm a lazy good-for-nothing lay-about." The brother had more insight than I had given him credit for. Lemoine whispered more confidentially than before, "He's a dumb-ass. Intelligence does not run in *her* family."

Outside the front door I turned to Lemoine, indicating the broken furniture and junk he'd discarded there. "When are you going to get rid of all this shit?"

"Never!" He was surprised I'd asked. "It might come in handy one day."

"What – as landfill?"

*

I headed back to Francine's office. At the end of Lemoine's street, I turned right and ended up behind 'The Walking Man'. I'd seen him out and about when I was also pacing the streets. I offered him a cheery, "Bonjour!"

He responded, "Bonjour! Ca va?"

I was surprised. Based on my few observations of him, I'd made a certain assumption. He always walked with a consistent tempo, moving unshakeably ahead, unperturbed by what was around him. Therefore, I expected him to be aloof.

We exchanged pleasantries as we walked. A small dash of autumn's disappearing sun, forced us to cross over the street, so we could continue walking in it.

"My name's Dougay," I offered.

"Audric."

"Pleased to meet you, Audric." We walked on. At the next intersection, I said, "You know I've seen you walking several times these past months I've been living here." He didn't say anything. "Have you lived long in Nice?" I asked, offering it as a conversation starter.

"Yes," he replied. I thought that may be all he was going to say, however I was pleasantly surprised again when he continued. "I have seen you as well. You always seem to have a purpose in your stride – always seem to be going somewhere of importance. Except the times I've seen you walking late at night, half-drunk. Then you stumble and sway more than walk."

I laughed. I had never seen him at night. Clearly, he had a greater awareness than I had.

"Do you like walking?" he asked.

That's an odd question, I thought. "It's okay." I went on to explain. "I have no choice. It's sometimes the easiest, and certainly the cheapest way to get around. I do a lot of odd jobs for people, so I seem to be often on the move."

He nodded, understanding, and we walked on.

"I go this way, Audric." We stopped.

He shook my hand. "Sometime, we should do this again," he said.

"Yes, I'd like that," I replied genuinely, for I'd enjoyed our brief encounter. I often get a sense of a person immediately, and I felt this old man might be worthwhile knowing. I turned to go – however I stopped on his voice.

"Dougay, you seem to be a man of the world." I doubted that. "How is it that some women seem to gather inner strength as they slowly break their man's heart?"

Chapter 2

I continued on to Francine's office, towards the Old City. I turned into Rue Beaumont, and walked up the stairs to the third floor of the familiar stone building.

"Was there any trouble?" Francine asked with concern, the light through the slats of the venetian blinds casting alluring shadows across her face.

"No more than last time," I said, avoiding detail.

"I'm sorry for that. He has a disrespectful attitude. Were there fisticuffs again?" she asked, looking closely at my face for any tell-tale signs. I merely smiled by way of answer. I showed Francine the photograph on my mobile. "Nice smile," she said, nodding approvingly, "for such an ugly face."

I scoffed as I bounced the photograph of Lemoine accepting the document over to her mobile. Opening her desk draw, she removed her purse, reached in and handed me an extra fifty. I waved it away.

"No need, it's okay," I said, gallantly.

"Dougay, take it. Your career, as Claude's dish washer, will not last forever." Francine has a way of saying things which resonate.

I smiled and left. I was unable to conceal in that goodbye smile the half regret, the flickering feelings I still held for her.

I walked down the three flights of stairs. On the street I thought of the words of the departing Audric. *How is it that some women seem to gather inner strength as they slowly break their man's heart?*

Had Francine somehow gained inner strength from our break up? No, I didn't believe she had. She was the same now as when I first met her. She had always been self-assured, knowing exactly what she wanted. Gaining inner strength from me? No, I was not that important to her.

As I walked, I kept thinking about how deeply serious that question was. Was Audric a philosopher? He was certainly well educated – far better than me. The fact that he asked me, and in the process exposed a little of himself, didn't bother me. After all we were strangers and strangers will often tell each other personal things that even their closest relatives don't know. What bothered me was the statement itself.

Trying to grasp what he truly meant, I thought of the few women, back in Australia, I'd had had an extended relationship with. I'd never felt that way about any of them. I guess I blindly loved them too much. That is a deficiency in me, for it had certainly been the case with Francine, and this awareness was the reason I was taking my time with Mary-Anne. The fact that the Atlantic Ocean sat between us was also helping.

As I walked on, I was still unable to let Audric's question go. How does one become stronger by making another person become weaker? Is there only a finite amount of strength in a shared bond and one gives way to the other and gradually feels stripped of worth? I had no idea. The only thing I was sure about was that Audric must have had his heart heavily broken over a period of time.

Once home, I pulled out the thick envelope from under the foot of my mattress. I'd never counted the money in there, so I simply slid in my two hundred euro. The envelope had been placed on my knee by Pierre Legrande, elder son of Madame Legrande, as I'd sat on her favourite bench in Place Mozart. I still couldn't bring myself to accept his 'reward', as I felt uneasy about it. It felt tainted.

Pierre Legrande controlled expensive high-class call girls, branded with a *fleur de lis* on their buttock, under his business name of 'Milady'. I'd found out who'd killed that beautiful blonde of his – the aforementioned Danielle Hubert. As I'd inferred, she'd been strangled by international movie star, Calvin de Marko. Several months later in America, Calvin de Marko had been killed in a head on collision with a truck. Pierre Legrande had contacts in the trucking business in America. You join the dots.

*

Saturday afternoon found me at Remy's warehouse for one of our regular sparring sessions. After knocking on the metal door, I heard him sliding locks and bolts from the inside, banging the roller door, pretending my arrival was causing him a great inconvenience.

Upon opening the single steel door, he said, faking disappointment, "Oh, it's only you." I threw him a mimed left hook and, in a flash, he caught it in his hand. It's very difficult to get a trick over Remy.

Remy Didion had been a professional boxer, however he had to quit when he broke his hand in the ring. He was years away from that required physique of the pro-fighter, however he was still stocky, for his body was built on muscle and sinew. His reflexes to the keenly trained eye may have slowed, though to the untrained eye they were as sharp as they'd ever been.

I'd been taught to box as a kid by a friend of my father's back in Sydney and Remy and I used these sessions as a way of keeping fit. Remy also used it as a way of feeling superior. We only punched each other's gloves, dancing and weaving about each other for thirty minutes. We'd pull any deadly blows we felt like landing on the torso of the other. In the time I'd been in Nice, I'd say Remy was the one person whom I'd call a true mate.

"Okay – enough," conceded Remy. I kept skipping and weaving, feigning his imaginary blows. I'd been tricked by him before. "I said – enough!" he said, forcefully. I didn't stop. He undid his gloves and walked away.

I slowed and dropped my guard. I looked about his warehouse. "You've got a new dining setting in. I like the red cushioned chairs." As I was assessing the dining suite, from behind Remy hit me lightly with his bare fist in my kidney.

"Hey!" I shouted. I'd fallen for another of his old tricks. I rushed him and pummelled him with imaginary blows. He laughed. I was too exhausted to join in.

Over the next twenty minutes, we sweated out the session and washed in the large sink, towelling ourselves dry.

"I'm thinking of going back up to Eze," he said. I stopped towelling myself. He saw the curious look I gave him. "I know, I know," he began, "there's no future there, but I really enjoyed talking with that woman – walking about her property, beneath the trees, a million miles from care. I can't forget her."

I tried to bring him back to Earth. "Remy, there's no future there. She's a lesbian, remember?"

"Can't you use her name?" He sounded indignant.

"I've forgotten it," I confessed. He looked at me, not believing what he'd heard. "Honestly – I have."

"Her name is," he began, making a point of my forgetting, "An-gel-ie."

"That's right – now I remember."

"Angelie Faivre," he said, with tenderness.

"How do you know that?" I'm sure I had never heard her family name spoken between us.

"I have friends," he said, lifting his eyebrows, teasingly.

I nodded. Of course, he had friends – and they all had their fingers in suspicious activities. I was sure one of them would have access to land deeds and land titles and to the names of who owned what.

"That time you and I were up there," he continued, "I really enjoyed my conversation with her." He was beginning to repeat himself – a sure sign of the beginning of an obsession. He saw my non-committal look. "Talking – that's all." He stood and stretched. "It can be wonderful talking with a woman, you know, Dougay."

I wonder why my friends think I've fallen to Earth in the last shower. Okay, I was new to Nice however I wasn't new to life. I wanted to say to him, *Yes, Remy, I too have had meaningful conversations with women.* I didn't. Instead, I said, "It's never too late to try. When are you planning on going?" He'd sounded urgent, so I expected he'd be off in his truck later this afternoon.

"In a week or two."

"You don't waste time, Remy," I said, dripping with equal portions of irony and sarcasm.

"Dougay, I'm a man of action."

*

Towards the end of the summer season, Claude had closed *L'Opera Mozart* early in the evening. It was Saturday night and I sipped my glass of water after my shift. Claude joined me. We were sitting in the dark, only the street lighting coming through the front windows allowing us to see the other.

"You're not your happy self, this evening, Claude," I noted.

"You are far too observant, Dougay." He sipped his water. If he wanted to tell me anything, I was prepared to wait. Eventually, he said, "Marcel won't be coming back."

"Ah." I couldn't have cared less about Marcel. Coming back or not coming back was of no interest to me, unless it meant that Claude would need a full-time replacement in the cafe. No, I reheard the disappointment in his voice and I realised Claude had meant Marcel wouldn't be back as a lover.

"Is his mother too ill?" I asked. Claude had said that Marcel was needed back in Marseille to take care of his sick mother.

"No." Claude shifted in his chair. "Dougay, over the past few months there's been pilfering from the cash register."

"You don't think I…"

"No, no, no. I trust you, implicitly, Dougay. You – I have known you for only what, six, seven months?" I nodded. "You exude an aura of honesty." He patted my knee, in a fatherly way. "Marcel – perhaps in that time he has acquired a drug habit – who knows? I've always been a little short – the accounts – at the end of each week."

"How do you know that? It may not be down to Marcel. You may have overlooked something."

"I know it because since you've been here full time, the cash register is no longer short." He stood and crossed to the bar. He turned. Perhaps in the dark over there he felt it would be easier to say what was on his mind.

"I love him. Yes, an old man and a younger lover. It just doesn't only happen in your world, Dougay. I was willing to keep turning the blind eye. I know, I know, an old man is a fool."

I wasn't going to say that. We've all been fools when it comes to matters of the heart.

"He won't return my calls. I can accept that he's found someone else, that's inevitable, I guess, though I never believed it would actually happen. I thought we'd be together – you know, forever." He paused, perhaps thinking of lost plans he'd made for the future. "He won't return my calls," he repeated, deliberately. "That's the part that hurts – here." He tapped his left chest. "It's as if I don't exist, or I'm unworthy of contact. He couldn't give me the respect of telling me face to face; nor via a phone call; nor in a letter."

There was nothing I could say. I felt his heartache. I'd felt that heartache before, when that young woman I once loved went off and married someone else. I'd read about her wedding in the newspaper.

Claude returned to the table and sat. "I can logically come to terms with it all – but it just hurts. He didn't have the decency to tell me face to face."

Chapter 3

I watched Claude leave to climb the stairs to his apartment above. I then left through the front door, pulling it locked behind me. Tomorrow evening I had an invitation to a birthday party and I'd suggested earlier to Claude that he might like to accompany me. I didn't want him to feel too alone, until he started to get his head together.

The next morning I began to sand down the walls in my second bedroom. The renovation of the original two small attic studios meant that what I called the second bedroom was actually the same size as mine and the removal of the second kitchen allowed the living area to be spacious. The bathroom down that end was untouched. I used it to store my two suitcases I'd brought with me from Australia. All my other worldly possessions, obtained through Remy's warehouse, were on display. I owned an uncluttered apartment.

After midday I filled the wall's imperfections. My plan was on Monday morning to give it the first coat, as rain was not forecast, and on Tuesday to finish it.

That evening I found Claude waiting for me outside *L'Opera Mozart*. He was nattily dressed, sporting a red bow tie. I had on my leather jacket.

"I hope you like slivovitz," I warned, as we set off.

"Why are we walking and not driving?" Claude wondered.

The birthday party was being held in the only Czech watering hole in Nice. The *Vlatava-Elbe* cafe, bar and restaurant, was over in the area around the port. I had a friend who treated the place as his second home. Milovic works as a luxury car chauffeur and it was his sister-in-law who was celebrating her fortieth. To be honest, the reason I'd been drinking water all week was because of this party. There was no way Claude was going to be able to drive his car home this evening.

Milos, the bar owner, saw us appear around the corner and shouted, "Ahoy! Hide the slivovitz! Dougay is here!" I waved. They were all gathered on the footpath, unaffected by the lack of summer in the evening air. Then again, they were from wintry Prague and I was from summery Sydney. They greeted Claude and me like long lost countrymen, sweeping us up in their bonhomie. With the introductions behind us, we all moved en masse inside the restaurant.

Claude knocked back his first shot of slivovitz and gasped, "It's not Pernod!"

"No! This is *real* liquor!" enthused Milovic. "Here – have a beer!" He thrust a cold bottle of Kozel Dark into Claude's hand.

The sister-in-law's name was Ljuba and her husband was Pasha. They did have a family name, though I didn't catch it above the noise. Even if I had, I knew I wouldn't be remembering it past 9pm. Ljuba looked like a younger version of Ulna, Milovic's wife. You could see why both men had married the sisters.

A Czech trio played lively music that everyone knew. It was probably a selection from the vast folk song and traditional music repertoire of their homeland. All the party goers sang along. Some of the musically gifted guests branched out into vocal harmony. We all clapped in time to the band, some banging on the counter of the bar beating out rhythms I never thought possible. And they danced. How *we* danced!

I was dragged up onto the floor by every woman in attendance. I had no idea if I was getting anywhere near the traditional steps that the others seemed to be dancing. My dancing style, my enthusiasm, my outrageous enjoyment of fun was driven by the famous choreographer, Doctor Slivovitz!

At one point, partners seemed to be changing and I ended up dancing with Claude. He passed me onto Milos who screamed, "Uurrgghh!!!" He passed me immediately onto Milovic who shouted at me that I had somehow ended up in the women's line!

After the dancing had stopped and the room quietened, a thick set man stood and sang a song so tragic and heart-felt that everyone was soon crying. Then everyone sang together in reply, with such vocal strength, such dignity, that I thought the room might rise up from its floorboards. They had to have been singing some patriotic song about beating the invaders, and dying for their country and flying to Heaven wrapped up tightly in their flag to their eternal reward.

Two waitresses in traditional garb were swamped on appearance from the kitchen. Milovic took me by the arm and we jostled our way through to one of the two young women. We hungrily picked up a piece from the tray. I have no idea if

Claude went hungry or not. When it came to acquiring food at a raucous birthday party, it was every man for himself.

Milovic explained, above the hub-bub, "Oblozene chlebicky!"

I bit into it as dancing makes me hungry. "Yum!" I said to Milovic, nodding my head in approval.

"Now you know why I have the figure I have," he laughed.

As with every party, it took a person's clapping of hands and raised voice to get the room quiet. There followed a few off the cuff speeches. Claude and I laughed, when the others laughed; and we applauded when the others applauded; and we raised our glasses in toast to Ljuba when the others did. And we gratefully drank whatever was thrust our way!

Parents with children made their way home and sometime in the evening there was a small group of us, wrapped in our coats, sitting around a table on the footpath. I guess we were all hoping the cold evening air would sober us up. However, that didn't stop Milos from bringing out a tray of slivovitz. Maybe he hadn't received the memo.

I could feel the blood beginning to pound through my veins. "That is not a good sign, Dougay," I said to myself. "Tomorrow, there will be a reckoning."

"Are you talking to yourself?" asked Milovic.

"Doesn't everyone?" I asked.

"No," said Milovic, handing me a dark beer.

I looked at Claude to see if he was still enjoying himself. He was stretched out in his chair, head back, staring at the sky, not moving. I leant into him. "They're called stars."

Without changing his position, he snorted. "Your jokes are terrible – and I am too drunk to move my head."

I noticed everyone was focused on Ljuba speaking, entertaining them with a story. When she'd finished, they laughed out loud.

"Milovic, what did Ljuba just say?" I asked.

Milovic and I always converse in English, as his French is basic. "Ljuba, four months ago, took a new job. She works as a nurse in the Clinique de Cote d'Azur." It meant nothing to me. "It's a private clinic." He asked Ljuba something in Czech. "It's a private clinic for – how do you say?" He tapped his head. "You know – crazy people."

"I understand."

"There's a man in there who always paints. Every day he paints. She asked him: *Why, Monsieur, do you always paint?* He replied: *God told me to!* Then from down the end of the ward, another inmate yelled out: *No, I didn't!*"

Ljuba leaned in to me and said something to her brother-in-law. She spoke in Czech, forgetting that she and I could converse in French.

Milovic explained. "Ljuba says that it's not always funny. This same man paints a painting which he takes three months to complete. Then he begins another. You know – seasonal. He is a very religious man. It's always the same painting – Mary with the baby Jesus."

"Madonna and child?"

"Yes, that is what it is."

I spoke to Ljuba in French. "There's nothing too crazy about that. It must be a good hospital you work at if he's provided with paint and brushes."

"He is probably from a rich family," she informed me. "They pay for him."

Claude was still star gazing and I thought it was time I walked him home. I took in a deep breath of cold night air and struggled to my feet. I said my goodbyes to the family, hugged Milovic farewell, and wished Ljuba 'Happy Birthday' once more.

Ljuba said, "After completion, the mad man looks at his painting for three or four days, rocking back and forth, side to side, gradually becoming overwhelmed by it. He then punches it – over and over again."

"Yes," I said, "Insanity is unfathomable." To her I nodded a smiled goodbye and wished her again, "Happy birthday!"

She added one more thing. "He only ever hits the face of the Madonna – never the face of the child."

Chapter 4

The painting of my unfurnished second bedroom went ahead as planned. I was pleased with the result. One day, when I'd finally finished all the walls in my apartment, I was going to paint all the skirting boards and architraves in white. Enamel paint can be a nightmare to work in. Grains of dust can lodge in the paint and spoil the smoothness of the coat once it's dry. When I finally complete that, I'll be throwing away the brushes. I don't want jars of paint riddled turpentine hanging around my apartment. Some beautiful woman may wander in here one day and I'd not want her to turn around and leave unimpressed!

Thursday morning Remy called early with a job for me. He needed help picking up some furniture. I walked under the railway line and over past the Russian Cathedral Saint-Nichols to his warehouse. He was waiting for me in his old white truck outside. I climbed in and we bounced off.

He parked in front of an apartment block near to the railway line. It was not a salubrious area. Two suited men waited for us. There were no introductions. Remy and I followed them up two flights of stairs, as the elevator had a sign on its door saying it was out of order. The hand-written scrawl could have been written years ago, as the ink was fading. The building did not have a high level of maintenance.

The two blank faced men knocked on an apartment door. It opened and they thrust a piece of paper in a woman's face. She staggered back and the baby in her arms started crying. A three-year-old ran to her and grabbed her around the legs. The men pointed to a small inexpensive circular dining table and four matching chairs.

Remy moved to it and looked at me, waiting for me to join him. I had not moved as I was not pleased with what I was witnessing. The young woman stood back. She was too fearful and too embarrassed to object, her two children both crying and clinging to her. She tried to soothe them, though her eyes were on the table and chairs.

"Hey!" called Remy, focusing my attention on the job at hand. I stopped thinking of the woman's plight and helped Remy lift the table down the stairs. The two men followed with two chairs each. They'd left the official document behind – unceremoniously tossed onto the floor. I could still hear the baby crying when we lifted the table into the truck. The chairs were placed in and we drove back to Remy's warehouse. It was a silent journey.

"Why are they yours?" I asked him once we were inside the warehouse and the roller door was shut.

"They're not."

"Whose are they?" I persisted.

"Who knows? The repossession men, I guess. I'm being paid a removal and storage fee. That's all."

"So, if no one is anxious for them, why not leave them back there with the woman who needs them?"

"The ways of high finance," he said, off-handedly.

Remy knew I was not happy with what we'd done. I paced and he waited for me to say something. Finally, I stopped pacing. "Don't ever call me to do that kind of thing again."

"It's got nothing to do with me," he protested.

"Don't call me!" I started to leave. I stopped at the door. I thought for a moment. I then walked back inside.

"Where are you going?" Remy asked, protective of his merchandise, watching me walk deeper into the warehouse. "Where are you going?" he repeated, louder this time, with a sense of warning in his voice.

I found the table and chairs I'd seen last Saturday while sparring with him.

"How much?" I pointed to them.

"Don't be stupid. You're not a good Samaritan."

"How … much?" I asked, deliberately.

Remy sensed my growing anger. "A hundred," he admitted.

"Fifty."

"Fifty?"

"Fifty and I waive this morning's fee." Remy said nothing. "And if you don't agree, I'll thump you."

Remy looked at me and smiled. "You've got me frightened now."

"Fifty! My waived fee – and free delivery."

"Come on! I'm not a charity," he pleaded.

I found fifty in my wallet. I slapped it into his hand. "If you're not prepared to drive, then lend me your truck."

"No one drives my truck except me!" He was affronted I'd even consider getting in behind its steering wheel.

Back at the apartment the woman stood back from her door as Remy and I placed the new dining table and the four red cushioned chairs in her living room. The babe was again in her arms and the young one was hiding, as before, around his mother's legs, afraid of us strangers.

"I cannot afford this," the woman said, apologising for her poverty.

I stood back and smiled, "No charge, Madame."

The young mother tried to refuse my offer, by waving away the dining setting with her free hand. When that didn't happen, she asked me, "What is your name, Monsieur?"

"Dougay – Dougay Roberre."

"God bless you, Dougay Roberre."

In the truck, Remy kicked over the engine and informed me, "You're a soft touch. One day it'll bring you undone."

I snorted. "Undone from what?" I swept my outstretched arm in a circle. "This glamorous and wealthy life I live?"

*

During the evenings of that week, as I washed dishes and swept the floor of *L'Opera Mozart*, Claude was up and down emotionally. I could tell when thoughts of Marcel dominated his thinking. On the positive side, he'd enjoyed Ljuba's birthday party. "I have never been that drunk since I was a young man," he confessed.

"Did they have fermented spirits back then? I would have thought you'd have gotten plastered on mead."

"Your jokes, Dougay, are for the birds – if they'd have them."

On Friday evening, sitting in the dimly lit café, Claude opened up. "I heard today that Marcel is riding a new motorbike around Aubagne."

"Where's that? I thought he lived in Marseille."

"It's a town east of Marseille, between here and there. It's where he's from. His mother lives there."

"So, that part of his story is true."

"Yes." He thought a little. "I doubt she was ever ill, really ill. I fear he lied to me. He had no intention of returning." Claude found two beers and put one in front of me. "Why can't people just be honest with you?"

I was unable to answer that.

"Where'd he get the money to buy a new motor bike?" I asked. "Did he steal a large amount from you?"

"No. Knowing Marcel he probably just wiggled his hips. He knew what he had and what to do with it. You understand?" I nodded. Claude went on. "The bike is probably courtesy of an old fool like me, though richer than a struggling café owner."

We sipped our beer. My mobile rang. I stood and moved away to answer it, for the screen read: *No Caller ID.*

"Hello?" I asked tentatively.

"Dougay?"

I half recognised the voice. "Yes?" I asked.

"Raphael. I got your number from my mother."

Raphael Legrande is the younger son, brother to Pierre. He did not dabble in call girls, for he is *un flic*. Upon hearing his name, I tensed a little, for I am not a fan of speaking with cops.

"Tomorrow night do you think you'll be hungry?" he enquired, obliquely. Both Legrande brothers loved to begin a conversation by easing around what they really wanted to say, rather than coming immediately to the point.

"Er...probably. What did you have in mind?" I asked, curious that Raphael Legrande was concerned with my dining habits.

He told me and I hung up. "Claude, have you ever heard of a restaurant called Le Grande Nice?"

"Le Grande Nice? I don't pay you enough to go eating there."

"No. I'm being taken there – by a cop."

"A cop? Order the most expensive thing on the menu."

*

Saturday afternoon I sparred with Remy. He threw a straight left at me, harder than usual.

"You're only interested in yourself," he said, as it hit my guarded open right hand. I had no idea what he was hinting at.

He hit me with a right cross, with such speed I nearly didn't see it coming. "Not everything revolves around you," he persisted.

Then he delivered his old reliable rapid left-right-left to the guts. I pulled in my arms and covered myself. "When are you going to ask me how it went?" he insisted.

I stepped back and dropped my hands. I shouted at him, "How *what* went?"

"I wondered when you'd ask," he said, with the timing of an old-fashioned comedian. He stepped into me. I raised my hands, and countered his forward movement by simply dancing back and to the side. "That's better – at last you're dancing," he said. "Where'd you learn that step?"

"I'm studying Czech ballet."

He laughed and dropped his guard. I should have taken advantage of that. I should have planted one right on his exposed chest. I didn't for his retaliation would have been unstoppable. "I've been to Eze," he stated.

I stopped moving. "Was she there? Or hearing you were on your way, had she managed to fly off to New York?"

"Smart ass!" he shouted as he hit my hands with his rapid left-right-left combination again and I once again danced a retreating step. I then stepped in and led with my left. I managed to keep him at bay with several repetitive jabs. I couldn't find a moment in his body movement where I was able to throw a right cross. We danced apart again.

"It was very pleasing," he confessed.

"That's it?" He had me intrigued now. "That's all you're prepared to say?"

"Okay, that'll do." He'd finally had enough physical sparring. He dropped his arms and stepped back. The session was over. "I didn't go," he confessed, finally telling me the truth. "Though I'm still thinking about it."

"Remy, I do not trust you." I dropped my hands and stood three metres from him. He laughed.

"No, no, no. Come closer. I promise – no tricks."

"Toss me my towel. I'm not going anywhere near you."

He tossed me my towel and we both removed our gloves. I watched his hands like a hawk. I knew when it was safe to approach him, as I'd learnt to see the moments when his body slid from its fighter's mode. I stepped towards the bench to sit.

Remy flicked out his foot and tripped me. I stumbled. He laughed.

"One day, Remy, one day!" I warned.

"Oh come on, indulge an old man."

"You're not old!"

We sat and sweated out the thirty-minute workout, washing ourselves in the large dirty sink.

I don't know what I do to some people, how I fill them with a sense of security, allowing them to feel safe enough to tell me their inner most secrets or ask me some crazy questions. Whatever I do, it can't be because they expect me to know the answers or be able to offer the advice of a sage. First there was Audric, then Claude, and now Remy.

He confided in me a question. "Do you think a man can have a worthwhile relationship with a lesbian, if he promises never to try to have sex with her?"

Chapter 5

I wore a pair of black jeans and my good leather jacket. As I neared the restaurant I saw Raphael standing outside in the doorway with the Maître d'. I heard him say, "Here he is. He looks like a criminal dressed in all that black." The Maître d' laughed. It wasn't the type of nervous laugh most restaurateurs shared with a cop. They were pals.

I followed them inside and the Maître d' lead the way to a table in a corner below a large black and white photograph of actor Yves Montand. I pointed to it and said to Raphael, "How ironic. By chance, your mother tells me she once kissed him."

"It's not by chance," he said. "Look about you." There were similarly sized and mounted black and white photographs of other French male entertainment icons. On the bottom of the frames, I read their names – Charles Aznavour, Alain Delon, Lino Ventura, Jean Gabin, Jean-Paul Belmondo. "We chose the photographs as an homage to her younger days."

"We?" And then it dawned on me. The restaurant was called 'Le Grande Nice' and his name was Legrande. "Isn't that name grammatically incorrect?" Even with my inability to read French, I knew the difference between *le* and *la*.

"Yes. But our family name is Legrande, not Lagrande."

"So, you own this place?" I asked, looking about at the sumptuousness of my surroundings.

"With my brother – fifty-fifty. We inherited it from our father. This is the only one of my father's many businesses I accepted. My mother suggested I bring you here. She doesn't feel you're eating well enough."

"Really?" I questioned. "I wasn't aware your mother took that much interest in me."

He laughed. "That's not the reason – though she did suggest I give you a treat – a belated treat for solving my murder case. What would you like to drink?"

"You choose – anything but slivovitz."

He didn't understand, so I explained my Czech connection. He ordered a bottle of very expensive white wine. I knew it was expensive because everything on the wine list was.

"Seriously, for a moment," began Raphael, "I want to thank you for what you did in finding Danielle Hubert's killer. I mean that, I really do. It would have been impossible to get that actor back here to face trial. Do you have any idea how uncooperative Americans can be when it comes to extradition? Also, here in France the pressure, from all those people above us mere mortals would have weighed heavily on Eloise Pittard's testimony."

I had found Eloise Pittard dumped outside my apartment building. I'd cleaned her up. She'd been savagely ripped down both sides by the fingernails of Belinda Swann, international actress and wife of Calvin de Marko. Danielle had the same scratches on her. I'd joined the dots for Raphael and his brother Pierre.

"Forget the political pressure," said Raphael, "the media attention alone would have broken her."

"And it would have exposed your brother's connection to her," I added. Eloise worked as a high class call girl for 'Milady'.

"That is of no concern to me. My brother has spoken to Eloise and she understands fully. She had no wish for a prosecution to go ahead and for her to be flung into the world's spotlight. Her occupation would have been used to destroy her as a credible witness. Who would be believed? A French whore or Hollywood's most famous widow?" He let the question hang there. "So," he said, "this dinner is a little thank you, my reward to you for a job well done."

We drank our wine and chatted. Raphael was a most charming host. I knew from where he and his brother got that.

The food arrived. I confess I have a fondness for oysters – natural, only sprinkled with salt. These were the first I'd tasted since arriving in France, for I could not afford them working as Claude's dishwasher. I did keep in mind his advice about ordering expensively, though I needn't have been concerned as even the bread roll here was out of my financial reach.

It was somewhere during my mouthfuls of Steak au Poivre, that Raphael asked, "What do you intend doing here in Nice?"

I looked at him, warily. I licked the peppered cream from the edge of my lips before answering. "That sounds like a police question."

"It's not meant to be. I'm curious, that's all. You leave a country you're familiar with and clearly still love and come to the other side of the world."

"I was born French."

"Where?" Raphael asked, with genuine curiosity.

"I do not know." Raphael studied me as if I was avoiding the question. "It's true. I left here about age three. My parents emigrated." I was not going to tell him they'd been placed into a witness protection program. I had no idea from where they fled and against whom they'd given testimony. It would be just my luck that it was against his father.

"To answer your question," I went on explaining, "I want to simply stay alive – for now, hand to mouth if necessary. I try to save whatever I can manage. I hope my future is very long."

"Save for an investment. That's my advice," he offered. "I know I had this place handed to me on a platter, so I'm hardly the one to speak of the struggle to save enough money to make an investment. However, as a young policeman, I did manage to survive without parental help. And my father being who he was – and my brother being who he is – well, I took the first opportunity to get out of Nice. I only came back here a few years ago. I'm at an age where my reputation as a detective is not tarnished by my family ties. This restaurant is perfectly legitimate."

I chewed a piece of steak in silence, looking around the restaurant. From the outside, the glass in the windows had appeared to be a smoky grey, however inside you could see through them onto the passers-by and the traffic moving out there. The tables were large, allowing plenty of space for the plates on the starched and immaculately ironed linen table cloths. The chairs were padded and comfortable. Gold railings and papered walls gave the feeling of warmth and security. It was my kind of place. The only thing stopping me being a regular customer was my lack of finances.

"You first joined the police force here in Nice?" I asked, my mind returning to reality.

He didn't answer. He looked at me as if he was feeling his way into a delicate subject. He cleared his throat. "I was impressed that you managed to track down Eloise Pittard and by deduction, figure out that that movie star had killed the blonde girl of my brother's."

"Danielle Hubert – you've already said."

"Do you still have that shrine to her?" he asked, a little facetiously.

"It wasn't a shrine," I corrected.

"Yes, I remember you saying. What did you call it? Yes – a 'memorial wall'."

I remembered only too well. I felt at the time that I was the only person who was missing her, and our paths had only briefly crossed.

Raphael paused, wondering how to go on. He began, "I too have a memorial wall – though I confess it is only up here." He tapped the side of his head. "My first case – forty years ago – it still puzzles me, as it was never solved. I was in uniform and attached to the detective investigating – an old school detective, charming, trustworthy." I doubted that. "Then before any resolution was possible, my application to be transferred to Paris was accepted."

"This case – what was it?" I asked, curiously. Raphael had hooked me.

"A baby went missing. I believe he was never found."

"A kidnapping?"

"Possibly. Or an abduction."

"What's the difference?"

"It may just be me," explained Raphael, "however, I feel an abduction is for the child – to claim it for oneself, or to sell it onto an already known buyer. I feel a kidnapping is for extortion – a ransom from fearfully anxious parents."

I appreciated his subtlety of distinction.

"There was no report of a ransom note, nothing to indicate anything suspicious. Vanished. Good parents, middle class. The father was a jeweller so the detectives suspected a kidnapping, but as I said, no ransom was ever asked for."

"So, an abduction," I concluded.

"Perhaps, perhaps. Who knows? Perhaps, it is too soon to say."

"After forty years?"

He smiled, nodding, accepting my point. He changed the subject. "I feel like some more wine. That okay with you?"

"Saturday night. I'm walking home. I won't say no."

Raphael Legrande caught the waiter's eye and ordered a second bottle. My apprehensions of an uncomfortable evening had evaporated long ago. I settled back once again. He possessed the ease and intoxicating spirit of his mother, in particular her ability to lead you through conversational strands, which could unravel or tighten without segue. Drinking the superb wine, I no longer cared where he led me for he was paying!

He spoke of some other cases, however not of a woman, a wife, or a lover who slipped away, or one he was now involved with. At the end of the evening I didn't know all that much extra about him, than I knew on the front doorstep when I'd arrived.

We did up our jackets to brace against the cool night air. I looked at the photographs on the wall once more. "President Mitterrand," I noted.

"Pardon me?" he asked.

"President Mitterrand is missing. Your mother has also kissed President Mitterrand. Your brother told me. Hasn't your mother ever said?"

"Don't believe everything a beautiful woman tells you, Dougay." He laughed. "Or for that matter, her elder son. Besides, in business, stay a-political."

The Maître d' opened the door for us and Raphael tipped him, saying "My regards to your wife, Maurice."

On the footpath, Raphael moved off. "Carvell Lefbvre," he said and then stopped walking, asking, "Where did that name come from?"

"Who?" I asked.

"The jeweller was called Carvell Lefbvre."

He walked away. I began to head off in the opposite direction. He called after me. I turned and we met again in front of the restaurant.

"The baby was named Donadieu."

I considered that, saying quietly, "A strange name."

"Think about it, Dougay. In English, *donner* means 'to give'; *Dieu* means 'God'."

"Ah," I said nodding. "Given to God."

He smiled, nodding at my comprehension and then moved off into the dark. I walked off in the opposite direction. I didn't get too far before stopping. I wished my comprehension had been working a little better back in the restaurant, instead of being dulled by the atmosphere, Raphael's generosity, and the fine wine. What was it with the two Legrande brothers? Why do they hide behind subterfuge? What was Raphael really after from me, telling me the story of the missing baby?

In my clouded head, I'd done a calculation and the numbers simply didn't add up. I figured Raphael to be in his early or mid-fifties. Forty years ago, he was not a policeman on his first job in Nice. He'd have been no more than thirteen or fourteen and still in school!

Chapter 6

"What were you thinking when you mentioned the back room?" Claude was draining the remaining glasses in the sink as I stacked the plates and put away the cutlery in the drawers – in the places I preferred, rather than the places Marcel did. It was time to submit my idea.

"I was just wondering if you'd ever considered knocking a doorway in the wall and joining that room to the restaurant area."

"Make the place bigger?" Claude queried. I got the feeling he'd been seriously mulling over the thought I'd planted. "I don't have the customers to fill it."

"No, but it would certainly look more appealing. Then perhaps customers would return more often and bring more of their friends."

"I cannot afford to do that." Claude was not flush with money, I knew that. The café was not running at a loss, though it wasn't thriving either.

I finished up and went home. On the way I made a small detour and bought some tomatoes and bacon. In my small kitchen pantry, I had onions, rice, a bottle of sweet chili sauce and soya sauce. Having been raised in Australia, there were many times I craved an Asian flavour in my food.

M'sieur Pom was where he always seemed to be, seated on his raised chair behind his desk in the foyer.

"You have a lonely look about you, Dougay. Are you happy with your lot?"

"Not only my mother, my father – now you're my social worker as well, M'sieur Pom."

"Look at this," he said, taking out this morning's newspaper from below his desk. "Remember you once asked about her – or him – I cannot quite remember."

He folded the paper over to a collection of society photographs, surrounded by a gossip column. He pointed to a particular one. "The Mayor with that same woman." I looked at it. The woman was Francine.

"That's not news." I brushed it aside. Francine no longer had a grip on my heart, I told myself.

"No, but that's not what caught my eye. Look in the background," he said, tapping the newspaper. "Who's that?"

I looked at the photograph more closely. "I have no idea," I lied.

"Ex-Deputy Mayor Deschamps." While I peered at the slightly out-of-focus man, M'sieur Pom went on. "I told you he'd not be out of the spotlight for long."

Pierre Deschamps had been involved in a scandal, caught in bed with a stunning blonde who was not his wife. The blonde had been Danielle and although I didn't take the photograph, I was there in the bedroom wrestling Deschamps's huge mongrel dog on the floor as the photograph was taken. I wanted to tell M'sieur Pom, for a laugh, that I hadn't recognized him wearing clothes. I kept my mouth shut.

He tapped the paper again. "You need a woman like her," he said, his finger resting below the smiling face of Francine. "It's not all summer here in Nice, Dougay. The winter nights are cold."

"Good night, M'sieur Pom." I walked off.

Behind me he added, "I could put an advertisement in the papers for you!"

Without comment, I took the elevator up.

I'd avoided it long enough – it was time to open the envelope Pierre Legrande had given me. In my bedroom I lifted the mattress and took it out. I sat at my small dining table and slid off the two hundred euro Francine had recently given me. Pierre's notes were all high denomination. I counted and recounted. I couldn't believe what he'd given me. Five thousand! I put it all back under the foot of my mattress.

I cooked my dinner, a concoction I called *Spicey-Ricey*, washed up and read my book in bed.

"One day I might buy a television set," I said out loud, flushed with the thought of all that cash beneath my feet.

I tried to go to sleep. My ankles couldn't relax. They'd never felt so much money!

*

In the morning I headed down to the sea. I was not intending to swim, merely walk along the promenade. Back in Bondi I'd swum occasionally in winter with the old guys, though the camaraderie was what got me into the cold water. Here in Nice I had no desire to swim in the cold water alone.

Up ahead, crossing a street, I saw Audric. I called his name. He stopped and we exchanged morning pleasantries. I walked for a while with him until I indicated that up ahead I'd be leaving him.

As I turned from the sea, he called out, "Dougay?" I stopped and he walked to join me. "Could I ask a favour of you, please?"

"Sure. Though I warn you, I don't have much money," I lied.

"No – not money. Would you like to walk up to the cemetery, out near the airport, on Sunday?"

I had nothing planned for Sunday. "Sure. Give me your mobile details." I punched his number into my phone. "Audric, I'll text you my number. We'll arrange a meeting time and place to set out from. Okay?"

"Okay. Thank you." A cloud came over him. He reached out and held my arm. "It's the anniversary of my wife's death – forty years," he confided. "This year I don't know that I'll be able to…"

"I understand. Major milestones always come with far too much gravitas."

"You are very insightful, Dougay. Until Sunday."

*

"It's a great idea, Dougay, but I just don't have the money for the renovation. Marcel, I'm afraid, has pilfered more than I realised." Claude was apologising, though there was no need. It was my crazy idea, not his.

I felt the moment had arrived – I was never going to get a better time. I'd been thinking of the dinner with Raphael and his views about investing, and I had that small nest egg under my mattress.

"Claude, would you be interested in taking in a partner?"

Claude stopped stacking coffee cups and facetiously asked, "You, Dougay? You wish to replace Marcel in my bed?"

"Oh, no, no, no! I meant a business partner."

Claude laughed at me and then said quietly, "Dougay, I am very wary of investing with strangers."

"Claude," I started, "I have a little money. I meant me."

Claude stared back, not believing that his dish washer possessed anything other than wet hands. He explained his reticence. "I have no idea how much a partnership would be worth. This place is not exactly an economic gold mine."

I knew that, though the cafe had space – and a back room. I remembered my father once saying that the greatest asset Australia possessed was space and that a lack of space constricts. He felt that space allowed for potential and *L'Opera Mozart* could sure do with a dose of potential. Just what that potential could be, I had no idea – yet.

"I have enough to pay for the renovation materials and a bit besides," I said to Claude, officially. "I'd buy in for five thousand euro." Claude said nothing as he sat back, considering this offer from out of nowhere. "And I'd do all the labouring – sanding, painting, knocking out the wall – free of charge."

He continued to think about it, tapping his fingers on the table top, before confessing, "I could never offer you much, Dougay. I fear I'm a poor investment."

"How's five percent?" I asked, taking a stab at a figure. I had no idea if it was beneficial to me – or him.

The offer of that amount and the small percentage in the cafe seemed to appeal to Claude. "Gross or Net?"

"Gross or Net – what does that mean?" I asked, my business naivety showing.

"Before expenses – cakes, beverages, wages – or after," he explained, as a father teaches his son.

"Do you own the premises?" My mind was now ticking over, calculating. "You're not paying rent?"

"I own the premises. I could be interested in five percent of the Net."

"That means 'after' – yes?"

"Yes – five percent after – it's called 'profit'."

"Okay by me, Claude."

"You are a blindingly honest man, Dougay. Are you sure – really sure?"

"Sometimes, Claude, you've just got to take a chance," I said, dismissing any second thoughts of foolishness I may have had.

He nodded. Maybe he'd taken a chance, years ago, when he bought the place. "I'm not saying 'no', but let me think on it," he said. "Is that okay with you?"

I said that it was.

I worked the rest of my shift without further discussion. Claude locked the front door and went upstairs to his flat. He returned with an old biscuit tin under his arm. When I'd finished stacking away the last plate, he beckoned me over to a table.

"These are old photographs of the place." He showed me one. I laughed. It was him as a younger man with a full head of hair.

"I looked alright, back then, didn't I?"

"That you did Claude, that you did. Though you were never my type." I think he was as relieved as I was.

He spread several black and white photos across the table top.

"Wow!" I exclaimed. "What's this?" I held up a photograph, though I couldn't get a bearing on where it had been taken. "There's an arch here!" I exclaimed. Claude said nothing. "It's somewhere, in here!" Claude pointed to the side board on the wall that held his best crockery. It was the wall which was shared with the back room.

"There?" I exclaimed. Then, not quite believing, I asked, "There's an arch *there*?"

"Yes."

I rose and went over to the side board. I stood on a chair and ran the palm of my hand over the wall above it. "It's been well plastered over." I turned back to Claude. "Why did you do that?"

"It wasn't me. The previous owners did that. They left me the photograph. If ever I needed to know the real structure of the building, I guess."

I climbed down, stood back and studied it all. I stepped slowly backwards until my back was resting on the locked front door. I didn't say a word to Claude. I didn't have to. He knew I was seeing possibilities. I sat back with him and changed the subject.

"Claude, you're never going to be your old self, until Marcel comes here and apologises for what he's done to you, face to face. I'm not saying to take him back. No. On the contrary, you're better off without him, though he needs to be honourable about it. He owes you an apology."

"That won't be happening, Dougay. I know Marcel far too well."

"I could go and get him and bring him back here to you."

"What – kidnap the man?"

"No. Ask him – reasonably."

"Forget it."

We sat in silence. Like everything suggested to Claude, I needed to give him time to consider it.

I rose and bid him goodnight. He let me out the front door and before he locked it behind me, he said, "I'll text you his mother's address."

Chapter 7

Aubagne is a commune, twenty kilometres to the east of Marseille. Overlooked by the bulge of the Galaban Mountain, its population, if you're interested, is over forty-six thousand. I was interested in only one of its population – Marcel Valiquette.

Remy stopped his truck outside the address Claude had texted me. I knocked on the front door. A middle-aged woman opened it, wiping her hands on a towel. She did not appear to have been recently ill.

"Bonjour, Madame. Is Marcel at home?" I asked in my most pleasant voice.

"Oh no," she replied without caution. "He always takes his morning coffee at *Cafe D'Accord*."

"That's *Cafe D'Accord* just off the main square?" I asked, lying through my teeth. I had no idea where the cafe was.

"Yes, but down the lane." I was surprised to find I'd been so accurate!

"Thank you, Madame." I walked back to Remy's truck. "Simple," I said. "*Cafe D'Accord*. It's off the main square, down a lane."

Remy advised, "Punch its name into your mobile."

I did. The directions came up on the screen. She hadn't lied. She was a trusting, honest woman, unlike her son. It didn't occur to me that she might phone and warn him of our arrival, for Remy and I weren't actually dressed as if we were knocking to notify Marcel he'd won the National Lottery.

Remy eased the truck into the narrow alley and stopped at an angle. With the front wheel on the narrow footpath, it took up the entire width of the laneway. Down from us three men sat at an outdoor table. Another man, wearing a beret, stood, leaning against the cafe wall. Of the three seated, one of them was Marcel.

"There he is," I said, pointing.

"Which one?" asked Remy.

"The young one who thinks he's a gay icon."

"Your boyfriend, then." I ignored him. "I'll watch your back," promised Remy.

As I approached, the man in the beret left the wall and walked a few threatening steps towards me, belatedly stepping aside to let me by, his eyes fixed on mine with his best thuggish glare.

"Bonjour, Marcel," I said, cheerfully, ignoring the beret headed man.

"What do you want?" Marcel snapped back. "Come to ask me which drawer the knives go in?" He laughed, derisively.

Next to Marcel, and between him and a bald-headed man, sat a dapper gentleman. He was finely attired and smelt of strong eau de cologne. I guessed he was Marcel's new love interest, the purchaser of his motorbike.

I explained clearly, not only for Marcel, but for the others as well, "Marcel, I'd like you to come back to Nice with me and to apologise face to face to Claude. He deserves that much."

"What?" shouted Marcel, incredulously.

"You heard. Claude's willing not to prosecute you for pilfering the cafe's money. It's a generous offer. No police involvement – just a face to face apology."

"And if I don't?" he asked, sneeringly. He'd tried to be threatening, however it hadn't come out quite the right way – too much 'mince' in his voice, I guess.

I turned to the dapper gentleman. "Monsieur, I'm assuming you carry weight at this gathering. Tell him I speak the truth. Marcel comes with me back to Nice, to apologise to his former lover, and then he gets the train back here. I estimate he should be back in time for an early dinner."

"And if he doesn't?" the dapper gentleman asked. "What if he doesn't go with you?" He spoke with an educated accent. I noticed a gold ring on both little fingers. The cost of a motorbike was a mere trifle to him.

"Then I'll be forced," I pointed to M. Baldy on my right, "To hit this bald-headed gentleman and possibly hurt him. You see, I gave Claude my word that Marcel would be back this afternoon. My word is my bond and I'd hate to disappoint Claude."

The perfumed gent eased back in his chair, confident, as if he thought he was in control. "But what if *I* do not wish him to go," he said. "You see, I call the shots in Aubagne, not you."

"Monsieur – it's a small…"

"Marcel is not going anywhere," the well attired gentleman said, with a smiling malevolence.

"So – fuck off!" shouted Marcel, gleefully.

"Monsieur," I began again, hoping he'd see reason.

The dapper man clicked his fingers. M. Baldy rose and stepped towards me. I jumped onto the balls of my feet and skipped into him and met him with Remy's speciality, a fast left-right-left into the solar plexus. That stopped M. Baldy's forward progress. However, I hadn't counted on the involvement of M. Beret. He smacked a chair onto my back, knocking me sideways onto a deserted table which, thankfully, broke my fall.

I heard a crack of fist on chin and the chair wielding thug hit the footpath at my feet, dropping the chair. As M. Baldy was lifting himself up, gasping for air, Remy hit him with a right upper cut into the guts, which sent him collapsing onto the cobblestones again.

I stood stretching my back. I hoped I was undamaged. Remy rubbed his left fist.

"Okay, Marcel." I breathed heavily. "If you'd be so kind as to come with us – into that white truck back there – we can be on our way."

I took Marcel under the arm and he stood without resistance. "Au revoir, mate!" I said to the dapper gentleman. I walked Marcel to the truck, Remy following, walking backwards like a commando exiting a jungle enclosure.

Marcel sat on the bench seat between the two of us. I spoke across him to Remy. "I thought you said you'd watch my back."

"I did. I saw your back get hit with the chair."

*

Back in Nice, Remy stopped his truck outside *L'Opera Mozart*. I walked Marcel inside. It should be easy to say 'I'm sorry', however Marcel found it very difficult. Like many people, he felt humiliated to be made to utter it.

You could have sliced the silence with Lemoine's tart's knife, for Marcel didn't speak. He stood staring at the floor in front of Claude, who had the look of forgiveness in his eyes. I hoped Claude wasn't going to tell Marcel that all was okay and he could come back and things would be once again the way they were.

To his credit, Claude held himself together. Finally, Marcel uttered something.

I said, "Claude didn't hear that."

Marcel shouted, in anger, "I'm sorry!"

I walked him to the door. "Within the hour there's a local train back to Aubagne."

Chapter 8

Cimitiere Caucade is situated south-west of the city, a little north of the airport. On Sunday morning as arranged, I met Audric on Promenade des Anglais and we headed away from the city, following the signs to Caucade. It was a fair walk, well over an hour, and I offered to pay for a taxi ride back to the city on our return. Audric said it wasn't necessary as there was a tram back to Jean Medecin from Ferber, a twenty-minute walk away. I said I'd buy the tram tickets. He laughed something about 'generosity' and kept walking. I tagged along behind, as we turned from the sea and began our climb.

Like my Sinatra song, I got a kick out of walking up Avenue des Eucalyptus, though I didn't see any koalas in the trees. At a school the street made a half s-bend and we crossed over a busier road towards a child's playground. Turning up hill to the right, we walked beside a high thick green hedge before coming to a formal entranceway.

It was an old cemetery, full of heavy looking headstones and family vaults and mausoleums. Like all cemeteries, upon entry, a cloud seemed to descend over one's thoughts, subduing any feeling of gaiety. The crunch of light gravel beneath our feet, along with the distinct lack of conversation, underscored the silence.

Obviously, Audric knew where he was going. The further in we went, the more paces I dropped back from him, wishing to give him space to pay the respects he needed to make. He stopped ten metres in front of me. He stood, head bowed. He was speaking over the grave, though I couldn't hear the detail nor did I wish to.

I wondered if anyone famous had been buried here. I did an internet search on my mobile. There were, though I confess my ignorance, as I didn't know who they were. There was a painter, Romaine Brookes who lived to be ninety-six; Rene Gosciny, a cartoonist; and Maurice Jaubert, a composer of film and concert music, who died in 1940. He'd been fatally wounded after blowing up a bridge.

I find headstones fascinating sources of detail, and diversions. They allow my mind to wander to another time; to suppose of the lives the dead lived; to…

Audric seemed to go a little weak at the knees. I stepped in quickly and held him from falling backwards onto the ground. Easing him from the grave, we sat on a nearby bench.

"Sorry," he apologised.

"No need, no need," I consoled.

"I do not know what came over me."

We sat there, the only sound his measured breathing.

The sun was having no effect on the temperature of the wind from the sea. I turned up the collar of my goat herder's jacket. The breeze didn't seem to bother Audric. He was miles away thinking of his life lived with his wife and of his longer life lived without her.

After we'd sat there for fifteen minutes or so, he simply said, "She'd often sit in our living room, towards the end, with a cushion over her face, gently rocking."

I didn't comment, though that image did not leave me. I hardly noticed a family passing by on their way to their loved one's grave, further in and over from us.

From out of the silence Audric asked, "What was she shutting out? Me? Was she shutting out *me*?" He tilted his head back. "I'll never know." There was a tear in his eye. From his pocket he took out a handkerchief and lightly wiped it away.

"It's as if she wanted to smother herself – rob herself of air. I suppose she wanted to stop the mental torment, the inner pain she was suffering. How can you see into another's mind, know exactly what is going on in there? I do not know and I cannot say. Only she can say what she was trying to do." He looked at me. "And she won't be saying anything about it today," he added with heartbreaking irony.

He put the handkerchief away, stood stretching his bones, and moved back to her grave. I moved with him and held him by the arm. Her gravestone read: *Babette Paquet*.

I now believed that she was the woman who'd gained inner strength by slowly breaking Audric's heart. I looked again at the gravestone. Yes, forty years ago today she had died.

*

On the tram, heading back to the city centre, I suggested to Audric, I'd buy him a coffee and slice of cake. It wasn't that I didn't feel he was capable of looking after himself, I merely felt he still needed to be with someone, anyone. It was too soon after leaving his wife's grave to return to his life of solitude.

"You're early," said Claude and then saw I was with someone and knew immediately I was a customer, not an employee. Audric and I were the only ones in the cafe.

"Why this cafe, Dougay?" he asked, curiously.

I explained how I work here and that I was hoping to buy into it, for a five percent return. "I'd buy a larger share however I'm not a millionaire, Audric."

The old man smiled knowingly. "It is admirable of you, Dougay."

I introduced Audric to Claude and ordered coffee and cake for us. We sat inside. Claude had an overhead heater on which made the place snug. The coffees arrived and I waited for Audric to speak, as I was in no hurry. After our morning in the wind from the sea, I appreciated the stillness and the warmth.

Claude placed two slices of cake in front of us and Audric cleaved a piece with his fork. He ate then wiped his mouth with the paper serviette.

"I still remember the first time I saw her. Ah, well, I'll never be able to forget that, will I? She was so beautiful, with a smile so radiant – and those eyes. What wonderful eyes." He sat back and drifted to a much earlier time. He looked across at me, as if for the first time. "How old are you, Dougay?" he asked.

"Ah, me?" I paused. "I'm forty one – or forty two."

"Don't you know?" he asked curiously.

"To tell you the truth, I don't. I don't know exactly. I have a passport which tells me I'm forty one." He looked at me, puzzled. "When I was three my parents had to leave France and go into protection. I simply don't know if my documents are absolutely real. So, let's say I'm forty-one."

"To where did they go?" he asked formally.

"Australia."

He nodded and sipped his coffee. He seemed to be calculating, thinking deeply as if doing difficult mental arithmetic. Perhaps he'd returned to the first time he'd seen Babette; the first time he'd held her in his arms; the first time he'd danced with her; the first time he'd kissed her.

He cut another slice of cake with his fork. As he ate, he studied me in detail. I smiled, a little embarrassed, and asked if he'd like another coffee. He said he would and I indicated to Claude that we'd both like a refill.

"She worked for my father. He asked me why I was always hanging around the shop. I'd never taken much interest in his work. However, from the moment I saw her, I started to. We married. Has anyone ever been happier than I was on my wedding day? I think not."

Claude placed the two coffees in front of us. Audric sipped, unconcerned by the heat. I blew onto the top of mine.

He put down his cup. "Then…" he clicked his fingers. "Overnight she seemed to change. From a very loving woman, she became distant, aloof. We still had sex, though it was never the same, then even that dried up. I never stopped loving her though. I hoped one day she'd snap out of it. I was more than happy to invest the time for her to grow out of it, at her own pace. However, one day she put a handkerchief over her eyes and walked in front of a car."

What can one say in reply to that? I sat, stupefied. Audric had revealed a tragic memory and all I had to compare it to, was a paltry memory of a young woman whom I'd fallen in love with, and upon hearing that, turned around and married another man. What could I offer, which in any way, could console him? How could I understand the heartache he continued to live? I felt useless, incapable of addressing his pain.

So we sat there, neither of us moving. After a while he smiled apologetically. "Thank you for the coffee, Dougay."

"Will you be all right to get home?" I asked with concern.

"Yes. I'll be fine." He paused and thought. "I didn't realise that sometimes it's alright to talk of things. It doesn't make them any better; it doesn't make them go away; it just – I don't know – offers a momentary release?"

I nodded as if I understood. He gripped my hand. "Thank you for your assistance today. Your ear has been most comforting."

Audric stood and moved to the door. "Dougay, sometime soon, why not come and visit me at home. I'd like to repay your kindness."

I couldn't say no. He opened the door and I watched him go. I formally said to myself, because I felt somehow, he deserved it, "Au revoir Monsieur Audric Paquet. A bientot, Mate!"

*

I tidied up the bar area and finished the washing up in the kitchen. I was drying plates and sliding them into their drawers when Claude said, "Okay. I've made a decision. If you're still interested, then I agree, Monsieur Five Percent."

"Hey!" I shouted in glee. I hastily dried my hands and we shook.

"I'll talk to my solicitor," began Claude, "and we'll get the necessary legal papers drawn up. You know her. When you were first here, I recommended you to do some work for her – Francine Delange."

Know her? I didn't go into any details.

Chapter 9

Claude and I sat opposite Francine in her office. Her young secretary had been surprised to see me walk in as a 'client' and not an 'employee'. Claude explained everything to Francine.

After that she studied me, and said, "Monsieur Roberre, it is pleasing to see that you are thinking of your future." I looked about the room to see to whom she was speaking.

"So, the five thousand euro and the labour costs will constitute the five percent of net profit? Yes? I am correct in all of that?" she asked.

Claude and I simultaneously said, "Yes."

Francine, making notes on a yellow pad asked, "So, have you budgeted for the legal expenses?" She looked directly at me. "To whom will I send my account?"

I hadn't thought of that. Claude looked at me. It had all been my idea, not his, and the look in his eyes underlined that point. I also got the distinct impression that Francine expected me to come up with those costs as well. No matter what the costs would be, and I was convinced they were not going to be minor, I didn't have them. Francine sensed as much.

"Claude," she whispered, leaning forward over her desk, "would you wait outside, please?" He stood and began to leave the office. Francine noted the look of concern and disappointment in my eyes as I realized the beginnings of my chance to become a capitalist had just stepped back, out of reach. "Claude, perhaps, you could continue on home," she began to explain. "I think I'll need a while with Monsieur Roberre."

Claude thanked her and left, closing the door behind himself.

Francine lifted her finger to me, indicating I should sit there and be quiet. She looked at the clock on the wall behind me and took out her mobile. Once the call was answered, she spoke Italian into it. Not long after she hung up.

"I didn't know you spoke Italian." I was impressed.

"Yes, but not English. It's fortunate you do." She placed her hands across her chest highlighting the shape of her breasts under her blouse. I wished she wouldn't do that.

"Is this what you really want to do?" she asked. "Buy a minor share in a café?"

"Yes, I believe so," I replied honestly. "I only have the five thousand and I need to look after my future."

"Five thousand will not buy you a very long future."

"It's a start. I believe in saving for a rainy day." That cliche was all I could offer by way of reason.

"Dougay, I'll be honest with you, I can waive the fee. I can draw up the contracts and not charge you a cent."

I sat back, fearing I knew where she might be going with this and where I might be going – like back escorting her home on Friday nights!

"I'm not a gigolo," I said, cautiously. To my ear it sounded as if I was unconvinced. I'm sure it sounded the same to her.

"No. I don't want a gigolo. I want you – again. You have talents I need."

I was unable to reply. I just hoped she didn't say anything further that might rattle my heart; anything that would make me yearn for her again; anything to make me feel empty inside when I left her apartment in the grey dawn; anything to make me confess drunkenly into her apartment intercom late at night ...

"It's a business deal – you understand?"

I understood. I had a choice to make – financial or moral. I could pay her the money or have sex with her. I had no money to pay. I had plenty of the other to give.

"What's the deal?" I asked, not that I needed much clarification.

"This Friday, Saturday, Sunday."

"I'm not a porn star!" I exclaimed. "I need to have my rest."

She laughed. "Are you free?"

I thought about the dilemma she was offering me. *Mary-Anne – forgive me. Mary-Anne – you'll understand, won't you? Mary-Anne – I'm only a weak-willed male!*

To make love to a woman, for a five percent share in a café, or not make love to a woman. That is some question! And when the woman was Francine, then the question was loaded!

I gave in to Francine's offer.

"You'll need to pack a bag and bring your passport or French visa or whatever foreigners require to cross over the border into Italy."

*

It was late afternoon and *L'Opera Mozart* was nearly deserted. A regular customer, I only knew as Old Hector had dropped by an hour ago and I'd been chatting outside with him, until he felt it was time to wander off home. As he did so, Monsieur Degas from the fourth floor passed. We said, "Bonjour," to each other and after a brief chat he wandered off as well. I picked up Old Hector's used coffee cup and walked it inside.

"Claude, I can't work for you on Friday, Saturday and Sunday. I need to go to Italy."

Claude stopped wiping the counter top. He dropped the cloth and stepped back, leaning against the shelf behind.

"What's in Italy?" he asked. "I thought you're from Australia."

"Ah – an elderly aunt," I lied. "I'm getting a loan from her for Francine's legal expenses."

I hate lying. I hate hitting women. Since my arrival in Nice I'd begun doing both. They say travel changes a man. I think they meant for the better, not the worse.

*

On Friday morning, early, I stood inside Gare de Nice. I wore my goat herder's jacket and old faded blue jeans. I had a suitcase with me. I'm sure passers-by believed I'd stolen the suitcase.

Through the window I saw Francine climb from a taxi and the driver lift her suitcase out of the trunk. She looked like a film star or model. Her light grey trench coat was tied tightly, highlighting her figure, over black leather pants. She wore dark glasses, her jet-black hair covered by a bright blue scarf.

She seemed to be in her own world as she moved towards the station. Those passers-by who were suspicious of me, must have got a real surprise when she walked up and kissed me lightly on both cheeks, escorting me through the ticket barrier, scanning both tickets and smiling to the railway security man on duty. I felt like a kept man. Then again, this weekend, why should I feel any other way?

We took the local train east to the Italian border.

Two stops on at Villefranche-sur-mer I squeezed her hand. She squeezed it back. Maybe she'd also remembered our one Sunday afternoon there, on the narrow sandy beach. In the water below, we had laughed and swam, both honestly happy with each other. It was from a time before I'd cruelled the wonderful Friday night arrangement I'd had with her.

After a brief wait in Ventimiglia at the border, we boarded the train to Milan. I was thankful Francine was taking me out of town for our dirty weekend. I knew no one in Italy, so I felt more comfortable with the idea. I held her hand once more as the train pulled out and headed north. She didn't push my hand away.

Was this weekend going to be the stuff of dreams?

*

Stazione Milano Centrale is a terminus, like Central Station in Sydney. It is the largest railway station in Europe by volume, and as we alighted from the train, dragging our suitcases, I understood why. People were everywhere. I was thankful it was nearing winter and I wasn't experiencing this feeling of being overwhelmed at the height of the tourist season.

Francine knew where she was going – I guess she'd been here before. I followed. After the ticket barrier, she headed left through people, past shops and kiosks and more people. I thought she was going to hail a cab. No, we dragged our bags through their parking area and over the gutters and driveways, to an intersection beyond, where we turned left into Via Mauro Macchi.

Down the street a little way, she pushed a button in the wall next to a door. There came a clicking response. She pushed against the heavy wooden structure and I joined in, helping her open it. We dragged our luggage into a small foyer and a very helpful young man took her credit card. They conversed in Italian. He was asking lots of questions and she was nodding and saying, "Si" a lot.

I stood by the reception desk as Francine went with him to a door off the foyer, against the far wall, marked 'Exit'. They conversed there for a moment. It was as if she was reassuring him.

She thanked the young man, and tipped him in cash. *Must be some Italian custom*, I thought. *Tipping before check out.*

An old elevator, similar to the one in my apartment block, was up a small step to the left. On the second floor I struggled with the heavy iron door and we managed to get out onto the small landing. She put a key into the door immediately in front of us. We walked into a large, living area, with a small kitchen against the right-hand wall.

I took my goat skin jacket off and tossed it onto the lounge.

From the bedroom, she turned to me and said, "Go to the toilet. I don't have too much time." I assumed she was desperate for me to begin to pay the fee then and there. She saw my look. "No. We have to go out immediately."

I did as she said and we walked back to the taxi rank and climbed into one. She spoke to the driver and off we went.

After twenty or so minutes, she paid the driver and we walked into a building. Francine became a tourist guide for my benefit. It was the rear public entrance to Galleria Vittorio Emmanuelle II, an up market shopping mall, the like of which I'd never seen. She walked me through, across the intersection of four large aisles and out onto Piazza del Duomo. I stood transfixed. To my left was the Cathedral. I'd seen pictures of it however nothing matched seeing it in reality, its jagged spires reaching to Heaven.

Was this reality? A long weekend, spent with a highly desirable woman, in Milan? There were worse ways to work off a debt, I reasoned. I have to admit, I was now comfortable with it – so much for my ethical morality. Long ago I'd accepted the fact that I am a flawed specimen.

I started to cross the large piazza, through the throng of people, to the Cathedral's entranceway.

"No," Francine said, holding me back. "Tomorrow we'll go inside." She took me by the arm and led me back inside the shopping arcade. She stopped outside a menswear shop. "Do you see anything you like?" she asked teasingly.

"Come on," I said, knowing there was nothing inside I could afford to buy. "There might be a cheap red wine around a corner out of here, somewhere, where I can treat you."

She smiled and pushed open the door to the menswear boutique. I stood waiting for her return, shuffling feet, for I felt I did not belong inside. In there she was speaking Italian to an exquisitely groomed gentleman with silver, slicked back hair. She turned and beckoned. I entered, cautiously, out of my depth.

Francine came to me and whispered, "I just told him that my husband has had his luggage stolen from the train and that he needs a complete outfit for tomorrow night's important business meeting."

"Is there an important business meeting tomorrow night?" I asked. Reality had left me some time ago, for I was now living in a dream.

"Of course," she said. "Why do you think I've brought you to Milan?" I tried to answer that. "Oh Dougay," she cut across, reading my mind, "I can have sex with you back in Nice."

She spoke again to the man and he removed my goat skin jacket. He said something to me. Francine translated. "He is wondering if you'd like him to burn it."

I laughed. What else could I do? "Francine I can't afford to buy …"

"It's all on me," she said, dismissing my concerns.

"How can I repay a debt, when you keep blowing out that debt?"

"All will be explained."

The gentleman ran a tape measure over me and inside of forty minutes I had two suits off the rack – a dark grey and a trendy blue; two matching shirts; and a pair of patent leather shoes. I could not begin to calculate the expense.

They were all packed into large plastic, branded shopping bags. I went to put on my old sheepskin. The gentleman spoke, stopping me.

"He's just suggested an overcoat," translated Francine. "An excellent idea – come on over here."

I followed. At first sight I fell in love with a pure wool dark navy three-quarter length coat. The gentleman folded it and packed it. Up until then I'd been the clothes horse over which Francine had flung garments without a say in the matter. However, now something caught my eye.

Francine said to me, "He's going to give you two free pairs of black socks. For the amount of money we're spending I thought he could have offered three pair." She laughed and went to pay at the counter.

My eye was still taken. I walked over and tried on a dark blue fedora. I tilted it to one side of my head, as I looked in the mirror. I repeated the gesture that I'd seen Philip J. Phillips do on the promenade in Nice, when I'd given him the final line to his movie, which subsequently became its title. Looking at myself, with the dark hat tilted over my left eye, I said quietly with an American accent, "Au revoir, mate!" I clicked my thumb as a trigger.

"Wow!" said a surprised Francine. She called back to the salesman. "We'll take the fedora as well!"

*

There was a price to pay – a most enjoyable one. Back in our hotel suite, we dumped the packages of clothing onto the lounge and Francine dragged me into the bedroom. I didn't resist.

I confess, I heard that famous song in my head and so I kept my fedora on. Francine laughed. I'd never heard such laughter during love making. It was the laughter of pure joy. It didn't take me long to join in the chorus.

*

"Do you know anything about a child's kidnapping, forty years ago?" I asked Francine, lying relaxed in her arms, as she stroked my forehead.

"Forty years?" She stopped stroking. "How old do you think I am?"

"I didn't mean it like that. I meant in legal circles. Is there anything spoken of a kidnapping cold case?"

"Why do you ask?"

"Detective Raphael Legrande planted its existence in my head. I suspect he wants to arouse my naturally inquisitive nature – to keep my eyes and ears open."

"How wide do they have to be, to hear and see something from forty years ago?" she asked, pointing out the monumental difficulty in the task.

"Yes, I agree. That's what I'm thinking." I let Francine go back to stroking my forehead. "The father's name was…" She stopped stroking. I thought carefully, wanting to get the pronunciation correct. "Lefbvre – Carvell Lefbvre."

"There's a jewellery shop in Nice called Lefbvre and Massenet," said Francine, "Though no one works there by the name of Lefbvre. If I remember correctly, Monsieur Massenet bought out Lefbvre years ago and Monsieur Massenet's children are all grown." I looked at her wondering how she knew. "I've done legal work for the second son."

I eased back down and let her stroke my forehead once more. Sometimes a man can't get enough of old-fashioned care.

"So, no old lawyers ever mention it at any of those Friday night drinks sessions you go to?" I asked, sounding as if I wasn't ever going to let go of it.

Francine stopped stroking yet again and gently pushed my head away. She thought for a moment. "No, I hate to disappoint you, Dougay."

"That's okay," I said. "You disappoint me in other ways."

I think she sensed what I meant, for she changed the subject. "I'm hungry. It's been a long day. What would you like?"

I thought about her offer. "How about hot pizza and cold beer?"

She looked at me. I knew she wouldn't go for it.

"Sure!" she said, eagerly. I often get things wrong. "I know a place."

I knew Mary-Anne enjoyed beer however I never thought Francine did. There was a sense of class about Francine, which at times she employed to distance herself from me. I'd been sure that she'd have relegated beer to us lower class types and raised champagne to her upper-class types, the types I felt she aspired to join and seemed to be comfortable with.

Pizza doesn't loosen the tongue, so it had to have been the third bottle of beer we were consuming back in the hotel room. Francine leant into me and took my hand. "You're a terrific lover, Dougay. You enjoy it so much."

Who doesn't? I thought.

She eased herself out from the table and crossed the room. She knew my eyes followed her. The way I felt tonight, they'd have followed her to Mars.

She turned. "I can never afford to fall in love with you. I hope you can understand that." I could only stare back at her.

She hadn't lost her touch for thrusting a dagger into my male ego. "Cheer up," she said. "We've the rest of the weekend ahead of us."

Chapter 10

I was woken by the ringing of Francine's mobile. I didn't move for the ringing had nothing to do with me. To be honest I was hoping to nod off back to sleep.

Francine picked it up and went into the living room and spoke quietly. She returned and climbed back into bed. I stirred and asked, pretending I didn't know, "Where have you been?"

"A phone call," was all she said.

"Everything alright?" I murmured, as if I was still asleep.

"Couldn't be better – just making final arrangements."

"Arrangements? At this hour?" The curtains were closed. There was no dawn light trying to sneak in.

"We're off to dinner tonight – a business dinner, remember? You'll need to wear one of your suits."

I closed my eyes though I didn't go back to sleep. She had not been joking about the business meeting. She had not been joking about needing me in a suit. The shopping excursion was not all generosity on her part – necessity had a great deal to do with it as well. Last night the pizza and beer belonged to my world. Tonight, I was expected to step up into her's.

We spent Saturday as tourists. We walked back through Galleria Vittorio Emmanuelle II, this time taking our time.

The man in the menswear shop nodded politely to me and greeted Francine in Italian, as if they were long lost friends. He kissed her hand, his eyes lingering on her. I felt he was thinking, *how could such a wonderful woman be with such a dead-beat of a man?*

Standing at the cross roads of the pedestrian avenues, I let the people hurry by. I studied the building above and to all sides of me, and particularly, I studied the exquisitely tiled floor. I would have loved to have done my bathroom floor in a similar design.

We entered the dark cathedral and stood, waiting to let our eyes expand to take in all around us, particularly the detail in the stained-glass windows.

In the afternoon, Francine hailed a taxi and we ended up outside an ordinary looking facade, with a nondescript entranceway. Tourists were lined up outside. She took out of her purse a sheet of paper and we headed to the guide at the head of the queue, who after glancing at it and scanning our internet ticket, pointed to a smaller line over by a doorway.

"When did you book the ticket?" I asked curiously.

"The moment you left my office – after you'd agreed to come with me."

"What is here? What's inside?"

She didn't answer. The queue started to move and we were led into a room. I looked to my right and on the wall was Da Vinci's *The Last Supper*. I stood and stared – and stared.

"Close your mouth," whispered Francine, hugging my arm, as if I was a small boy and she was my educating mother.

The guide began to deliver her church approved spiel. I didn't listen carefully, as my eyes were taken by the fact someone, sometime ago, had cut a doorway into the masterpiece. I shook my head and muttered, "Dumb, ignorant priests."

"Shhhh," whispered Francine. Yes, she was my mother!

The guide said something in halting English about the young apostle James and how it wasn't Mary Magdalene. She pointed to the mural and those apostles gathered around Christ. 'James' sure looked like a woman to me.

*

I chose the blue suit. I put on the overcoat and tilted my fedora on my head. I stood and waited in the entranceway to our room.

Francine came out of the bathroom and over reacted. "Excuse me, monsieur," she said, faking surprise. "Did you see where Dougay went?"

"Very funny!" I admonished playfully. She poked out her tongue and in that moment I saw the twelve-year-old girl – innocent and fun loving. She began to put on clothing. If she hadn't had, we were going to be very late for the dinner.

When she emerged into the living room, I felt we still could be late for dinner, as she had on her black leather pants and a bright silver blouse under a tight-fitting maroon jacket. Fully clothed or totally naked, some women just bring out the unforgiveable sexist side in me. With the image of *The Last Supper* still in my head, I heard one of those apostles around that dining table whisper, *Lust is a sin!*

We didn't leave immediately. "Pack your bag, Dougay." She went into the bathroom and returned handing me my toiletries bag. "Come on," she said.

Without question I did so and watched her complete her packing. From under my pillow she tossed me my kangaroo t-shirt. I'd forgotten I'd left it there. I put it in my bag. Dragging both bags into the living area, she left them inside, near the doorway. As we walked down the stairs I asked her, "Are we doing a runner?"

"Something like that."

*

The taxi dropped us outside a fancy looking restaurant. I glanced up at its name above the door. I had no idea what it said – *La something or other*. Francine paid the driver and I waited for her to take my arm. She didn't walk me inside immediately. She stood by me, looking about, as if checking for eavesdroppers.

She whispered, "Tonight, I really need you." Was she at last falling in love with me? "I really need you to hear everything that is said in English in here. Please, I beg you – pretend that you neither speak nor understand it."

"Sure," I said. "Anything you ask."

"I have met these Italian brothers, once before, in my office, back in Nice. Here, on their territory, I'm very wary. If they want to hide something from me, they speak in English. Just remember everything you hear, okay?"

"Okay." She nibbled my ear, kissed my cheek and escorted me inside.

*

Giovanni and Giuseppe Mascati were identical twins. In their mid-fifties, they were suave and elegant. Their short black dyed hair was gelled back as if their hairdresser had a fixation with old time movies. They wore eye catching finger rings and one of them had a gold front tooth – Giovanni, who when we joined them, was seated on my right.

As we walked to their table they stood, smiled and presented as if they were representatives of the Catholic Church, doing good will amongst the poor – spreading the word, though the word they offered the church was probably financial.

Francine and I were greeted with great charm and warmth – hands shaken and cheeks kissed. The brothers were too welcoming. I knew immediately why Francine didn't trust them. They each carried a disturbing threat of malevolence which they'd inherited from birth. Back in Australia, we'd have referred to them as *a pair of scum-bags*.

Like all people who must dominate, they'd already ordered for us. Giuseppe asked Francine something in Italian. She asked me, in French, "Are you vegetarian?" I replied I wasn't.

Then Giuseppe leaned into me and said in English, "People who don't eat meat do not know what they are missing." I didn't react, I merely read the wine list though I knew this evening I wouldn't be getting a choice. Giuseppe accepted my façade. It wasn't hard for me to look ignorant – that was the facial expression I woke up with each morning.

Giuseppe surreptitiously tapped his twin on his wrist. Giovanni looked past me to the doorway. A man walked up behind me and passed, standing between the twins and after leaning forward, spoke in English to his bosses.

"It is a pleasure to see you once again. Peter and Paul offer their good grace, and bless this meal. They are prepared and in place." He left again.

I gladly accepted the Antipasto. I gladly accepted the Pasta. I gladly accepted the Veal Scallopini. I waved away the desert. I didn't wave away the wine, which was a particularly good Frascati from the region south of Rome. I could make that out on the label, though I did ask Francine to translate for me, anything to keep those greasy haired twins in the dark.

After the dishes were cleared – I was pleased I wasn't scrubbing in that kitchen tonight – Francine took from her shoulder bag a large envelope.

She and the Mascati brothers eased in, forming a huddle. They spoke in Italian.

The two men shared Giovanni's gold pen and signed the contracts before them. Francine signed and then asked me to witness everything. The gold pen was real, for it felt weighty in my fingers. Francine kept one copy for herself and slid the remaining copy of everything to Giuseppe who held out his hand in anticipation. Giovanni, from under his seat, slid an envelope across the table to her. She felt it quickly, smiled warmly, and slid it into her shoulder bag. She asked me to remain while she went off to the ladies' room.

Giuseppe attempted once more to speak to me in English, leaning in and confiding, "A beautiful woman. If I wasn't in love with my brother's wife, I'd fuck her."

These brothers were clever. It was a very funny thing to say and designed to trap any English speaker. I did not raise an eye brow, though I did intend laughing about it on the way back to the hotel. Sipping the last of my wine, I put the glass down and pointed to it. I nodded my delight at having drunk such a superb drop and at their hospitality for having provided it. It was a very congenial moment in pantomime. We could have been old friends – three gentlemen of Verona.

Francine returned and said it was time we were going. I shook their hands and nodded so much that I thought I was back in my favourite Thai restaurant in Bondi, another Saturday night happily spent.

The man, who'd delivered the message regarding Peter and Paul, watched us as we waited on the footpath.

A taxi pulled up. I hadn't seen Francine hail it. We got in and it immediately drove off. The driver knew where we were going! Looking back, I saw the man outside the restaurant write something down on a small piece of paper, glancing up to check that he'd notated the taxi's number plate correctly. He then pulled out his mobile.

"Well?" Francine asked, "Anything to report?"

"The Mascati twins are very religious. Peter and Paul blessed our meal and are in place – whatever that means."

She curled inward her lower lip, assessing what I'd said. It must have made sense to her for she squeezed my hand and opened her bag, removing from it the envelope she'd been handed earlier.

"Stick this down the front of your trousers. Then cover it with your shirt. Do up your suit jacket around it." She passed the envelope to me.

I started doing as she asked. I pushed forward my hips and slid it in. I managed to sit back onto the seat once more, without too much discomfort.

"What's in here?" I asked.

"Cash."

Chapter 11

"Holy shit!" I exclaimed, feeling the bulky package with a greater attention to detail than before.

"No questions, Dougay. Keep it down your pants."

I took my hands off it. "So, babe," I asked in a drunkenly suave voice, "Do you wish to try and take it out?"

"Dougay, now is not the time to be flippant." I wondered when that time would be. I had on a new expensive suit and a belly full of the best food and wine. I was feeling exceedingly laid back and contented.

Francine set about ruining my complacency. "Sometime back, the Mascati twins tried a similar trick, on an old friend, to the one they're planning on pulling tonight. They intend robbing me, to get back their money. It's an old ploy. They paid the money and signed the contracts – everything legal. Therefore, the property they bought in Nice is theirs and they get to keep their purchase price, once they steal it back. And if they do, then I'm the one responsible. I would have to pay over – out of my own pocket – six hundred and fifty thousand."

"How much?" I gasped.

"You heard."

"I know what I have down my pants is worth a lot of money – to me, at any rate – but I never imagined it would ever be worth that much."

"Dougy – be careful when we get out. Look, I apologise, I've used you. Only you could do this for me. Remember the first time you worked for me? How you got Lemoine's signature? Well, I'm going to need that side of you tonight – soon, very soon."

The taxi pulled up. I began to give her back the money. "No. Keep it there. They'll expect me to have it."

I opened the rear door of the cab as quickly as I could and bounced onto the balls of my feet. Peter charged me and I hit him with the reliable Remy Didion special, that fast left-right-left to the guts, with much more savagery than Remy had ever delivered sparring.

Paul ran to me. I stepped to the side and as he charged, I helped him on his way with a savage left hook. I tried to hit the ear, as that would soften the impact on my fist. I was bang on target.

Peter came again, trying to throw a round arm right. I set him back on his heels with a straight left. It's an old-fashioned blow and mightily effective. Maybe these days, thugs expect you to leap in the air and kick them in the teeth. Not me. My feet were firmly on the ground. I followed the straight left with a classic right cross, and a left hook and right upper cut to the chin. Text book stuff – that's why it's in the text book – it works! I wrung my hand, trying to shake out the pain. I hate the impact of fist on chin bone.

I wanted to ask Paul if he was planning on having children, though I couldn't as I didn't speak Italian. I was planning on kicking him in the nuts, though being the caring person I am, I hit him above them, my third knuckle slightly extended. He howled as my pointed knuckle slammed into his groin.

I reached into the taxi and pulled Francine out. As I turned and stood up, Peter hit me in the guts – right in the middle of the six hundred and fifty grand. I didn't feel a thing. He wrung his hand. I planted another blow into his rib cage. He let out a "Phooor!" I didn't want to hurt my fist again, so I hit him on the back of the neck with a karate chop. He uttered something in Italian and fell to the pavement. I didn't think it was, "Forgive me Father, for I have sinned!"

Francine stepped over him. The cab took off. Paul was still rolling in the gutter and moaning, holding onto the source of his future children. I don't think he was thanking me for deliberately missing the bull's eye and thereby allowing him to one day conceive some.

Francine pushed the buzzer for the front door and after it clicked, we both pushed our weight against it. It opened, we half fell inside. The door shut behind us. We were home.

The young man was not surprised to see us. He checked the time on his mobile and said something to Francine.

"Yes," she replied in French, "on time."

He was expecting us! We followed him through the foyer to the fire exit at the end. He pushed it open and Francine dragged me out into a small courtyard.

"What about our bags?" I asked hurriedly.

"Come on," she said, dragging me across the courtyard to a small laneway opposite.

"What's going on?" I managed to say.

Without stopping, she said, "I'm a lawyer – trust me!"

"This is not the time for ironic humour."

"Come on." She dragged me onto the street behind. A taxi was waiting there. It was the same taxi – he'd driven around the block. We climbed into the rear seat again. She pushed me down and then fell on top of me. The cab crawled off, not arousing suspicion. From the outside it appeared as if there were no passengers inside.

After a while we sat up.

"I'll explain – one day." Francine laughed, more through relief than self-appreciation of her own wit.

"Those two thugs," I began to ask, "Peter and Paul. Did you notice they had similar moustaches?"

"No."

"It was like they saw themselves in some old gangster movie. They were freshly oiled."

"How do you know that?"

I held up my left fist. "Their moustache oil is all over my knuckles."

Francine took out a tissue and wiped my tender fist dry.

The cab stopped at the Holiday Inn out near the airport. Now, I finally knew why I needed the passport. We'd be flying back to Nice. I was with a smart woman. The Mascati brothers would be sure we'd go home on a return train ticket.

Francine paid the driver and he waved us goodbye. He said something to Francine and she laughed.

"What did he say?" I asked her, as the cab's tail lights faded into the night.

"He wants to know if you could take care of his brother-in-law for him."

We went inside and she checked us in. The room had already been reserved and our bags were waiting for us in the room. She'd thought of everything.

"Lay out your clothes for the morning."

"Why?"

She looked at me, and then with an alluring smile of happiness, she danced towards me temptingly. "Because I'm a woman – and therefore, you can trust me." This time I managed a laugh.

Francine kissed me on the cheek and I found my clothes for the morning. "Clean your teeth now – you won't have time in the morning." I did. "Pack everything away," she reminded me.

I finally slumped into a chair. It was as if the evening's excitement had suddenly drained from me. She opened the bar fridge and held up a bottle of beer. "Yes, please," I managed to say.

She handed the beer to me and then she started singing as she removed her clothing in an elongated strip tease. She was very happy. I don't think I'd ever seen her quite like this. Relief, I guess it was – relief that it had all gone so well; relief that she wasn't going to have to pay out of her own bank account six hundred and fifty thousand euro.

Trying to remove her tight leather pants she fell to the floor and we both laughed out loud. I didn't have the energy to go to her and lift her up.

"I can't get up," she laughed, splayed on the floor before me, her leather pants wrapped tightly around her ankles. "You can either take me here or wait until I get these things off and come over and climb all over you."

"I'll wait," I said with false nonchalance.

Somehow, all she needed was the incentive of me playing 'hard to get', for she managed to find her feet again. She swayed her hips at me and took the beer from me, literally out of my mouth. She drained the remainder of the bottle in one gulp. Then she climbed on top of me. She was uncomfortable there – she couldn't settle – for I still had the money wedged down my trousers.

"I've always wondered what it would be like to be seduced by six hundred and fifty grand," she said, as she reached in, tossing it away with me rising to the occasion.

*

Her phone alarm went off at 4 am. She pushed me out of bed. She pulled over my head my kangaroo T-shirt and tossed it into her suitcase. She then started dressing me faster than I could manage. "Come on," she said. "Hurry."

"What's the rush?" I asked. "There aren't any flights at this time of the morning, are there?"

There was a knock at the door. I froze. It was far too early for room service. I stepped quietly to the door to open it.

"No!" She hissed. I stopped. "I'll get it," she reassured me.

Francine indicated I should stand very still. She kept the door on the chain, opening it a fraction as she peered out. Immediately she slammed it shut. I clenched my fist and went to her. Ignoring my assistance, she unchained the door and reopened it.

"Jules!" I exclaimed.

*

Jules St Croix is a private investigator. I'd worked for him on several 'cases' Francine had sent me his way. I never knew whether to thank her for that or not.

Jules had taken the infamous photograph of Danielle Hubert servicing Nice's Deputy Mayor, Pierre Deschamps, while I wrestled Deschamps's savage dog who thought my name was 'breakfast'.

As quietly and efficiently as possible, Jules and I dragged the two suitcases directly to the car park. Francine joined us there once she'd settled the hotel account.

"This is not your car, Jules," I said as he drove up from the underground car park, into the pre-dawn dark.

"No, mine would not have made the journey."

We drove away from the airport. "Any chance we'd be heading to Nice, now? No train; no plane; is this car taking us home or will we begin hitch hiking down the road a way?"

Francine smiled. The Mascati cash was again in her shoulder bag and her arms were wrapped around it, hugging it to her chest.

The car drove on, the rhythm of motion sending me to sleep. I woke momentarily. "Where are we?" I asked.

"Still in Italy," said Jules.

Francine didn't answer for she was asleep, her head on my shoulder. I fell back. When I awoke, the sun was up and the Mediterranean was on my left. I breathed a lot easier.

"What day is it?" I asked.

"It's still Sunday," said Francine, now awake.

Jules laughed from behind the wheel. "Francine's been telling me how you masterminded the whole thing."

I scoffed. "I never masterminded anything! I hadn't known what was going on until it was well and truly over. Even now I don't know if I understand all of the details."

Francine took my hand. "You're my hero!" she exclaimed. Then she and Jules laughed again.

Chapter 12

"Jules," I asked, as he drove on, "have you ever heard of a kidnapped baby, Donadieu Lefbvre?"

He thought about it, probably mentally rifling through all those old files strewn about his cramped outer office. "No. When was this?"

"Forty years ago."

"Forty?" he asked, shocked. "I was a baby myself back then." Both Francine and I scoffed. "Okay, okay," admitted Jules, "I may have been thirteen."

"So – you haven't heard of him?"

"Never."

Once back in Nice, Jules pulled up outside Francine's apartment block on Rue Barla.

"Can you pass me my t-shirt out of your luggage, please?" I asked Francine.

"Come on, you're coming with me. The weekend is not yet over." How much did I still owe on those legal transactions?

I bid goodbye to Jules and thanked him. "Until we meet again," he replied. "There may be something coming up. I'll give you a call. It may amount to nothing, so don't lose sleep waiting for my job offer."

Before I could say, "You can keep your job offer," he drove off.

I dragged my suitcase behind Francine up into her apartment. Leaving it just inside the door, I fell into her lounge chair. We were exhausted. I think Francine fell asleep, stretched out on her lounge, for I know I did in her lounge chair.

*

Around 6pm her intercom rang and she answered it, buzzing in someone from downstairs. I went and stood by the window. Better to be on my feet than lounging in a chair if trouble walked through the door.

Her doorbell rang and she let in a well-dressed man, though to be honest, he was not as well dressed as I had been last evening. Francine shook hands with him.

"Bonjour, Paul," she said.

"Bonjour Francine, did everything go smoothly?" he asked.

"Yes. There was only a minor hiccup," she assured him, "which my assistant here took care of."

The man smiled at me and nodded his gratitude. "Those Italian twins are like leopards. They never change their spots." He spoke with a cultured voice, though I suspected some of his business activities weren't.

Francine handed him the package. He slid out the signed contract, glanced through it and nodded. He counted the money. I've never seen six hundred and fifty thousand counted before. If ever I stumble upon such an amount again I'll now know how to do it.

The man flicked off some high denominational bills and gave them to Francine. He shook her hand and left. Francine closed her apartment door.

"What did he sell?" I asked.

Francine weighed up whether to tell me or not. She decided to.

"Remember about five years ago, there was that printing press fire? Ended up burning down that small warehouse?"

"No. I didn't live here in Nice back then."

"Of course, I momentarily forgot. Well, Paul has finally been cleared of any wrong doing and he's off loaded it onto those Italian twins. God knows what they'll do with it." She walked to me. "It's just you and me now – finally alone – without me worrying about anything." She kissed me gently on the cheek and went into her kitchen, calling back, "Glass of white wine?"

"Yes, please," I answered, eagerly.

We clinked glasses. "So, Monsieur Roberre, you are now a five percent partner in *L'Opera Mozart*. You can collect the papers on Friday afternoon at 4pm. They'll be with my secretary." Francine was now once again the solicitor.

She saw the look in my eye and went on to explain. "I'll be out of the office all day on Friday – nothing that needs your services." She flicked her fingers, dismissively. "A very mundane matter – I'm announcing my engagement to be married."

*

I don't know how long I stood, stupefied. She waited for me to say something, however nothing came. Finally, with a touch of ironic bitterness, I said, "And you didn't even knit me a scarf."

She didn't understand and I didn't explain. She took me by the hand and sat me on the lounge next to her. It was as if a mother were about to tell her child a parable.

"Dougay – I can't live my life with you." She squeezed my hand, consoling me, as if I'd just lost a foot race or missed a crucial penalty shoot-out.

"You know the kind of person I was. You've seen the *fleur de lis* tattoo. I was never one of Pierre's girls – I'm far too old for that. I was one of his father's, though. In fact, I was his mistress. He paid me well and I put myself through university. Even then I knew I was not going to become a washed up, drug ridden, old whore. I attended every class they asked of me, and I submitted every assignment they asked of me, and I passed every test they set me. I was not the smartest student in my cohort however I was the hardest worker. I was a plodder who absorbed it all, and over time I walked and in my final year I ran. My nights may have been scandalous, but my afternoons weren't. I studied. After I graduated, Pierre's father set me up in my business – for one year only. I had to make a go of it and I did."

Though Francine didn't know, I knew she'd been old man Legrande's mistress, for Mary-Anne had told me.

"It is a failing within me. I have to keep climbing – climbing my way out of my childhood. This engagement will cement me in society. I can't stay with you – don't get me wrong, Dougay, I'd love to. You make me happy, for you are more like the real me than I care to be reminded of. That might be the problem. I want to wake each morning – there." She pointed upward. "Not there." She pointed downward.

It's an odd feeling having a beautiful woman tell you calmly and logically why you're not suited for her – that your life and prospects simply don't match her dreams.

"I need to be finally satisfied. Not sexually," she laughed. "He'll never satisfy me sexually. I've come to terms with that. I'm going back into a life of celibacy." Again, she saw the look in my eye. "He's gay."

I tried to say something. She put her finger gently over my lips.

"Please, you must never disclose what I'm about to tell you. Promise?" She looked deep into my eyes.

"I promise."

"The gentleman is Maurice St. Romain."

I'd heard the name. I thought for a moment and then asked, unsurely, "The Mayor?"

"Yes."

"These days, who cares about him being gay?" I asked. I couldn't have cared less about the Mayor's sexual preferences.

"He does. He has family connections with the first family of Monaco." I remembered hearing that – probably from M'sieur Pom, as he'd be the only person I knew who kept up with the Cote d'Azur's political machinations and familial connections.

"So, you're going to be a – 'smoke screen'?"

"Something like that," she said. "I'll be at last legitimately rubbing shoulders with…" She didn't finish. Perhaps the prospect of those shoulders wasn't as inviting as everyone believes. She took both our glasses to the kitchen.

I sat and took it all in, as I heard her rinsing the glasses in the sink. Francine had one final step to go, to reach what she'd always wanted. How many steps did I have? I didn't even know where I wanted to be, so there was no staircase in front of me I could possibly step onto.

She returned with two freshly filled glasses. I took a large mouthful. We talked over those things some more – she clarified her feelings and reasons and tried to soothe my feeling of self-worthlessness. After the third glass I stood to go.

"May you be as happy as you can be, Francine." I took hold of my suitcase and headed to her door.

"Can I keep your t-shirt?" she asked. I'd forgotten she'd put it into her suitcase back in Milan, and hadn't returned it to me.

"That old thing?"

"Yes, I'd like to."

I shrugged, "Sure." I turned to go.

"I'll remember you every time I see that kangaroo on the front of it."

I turned the handle on her door. Her voice stopped me leaving.

"Don't you need me to sign your letters of agreement?" she asked. "They are no good to you without my signature on them. They just need to be finalised."

I looked back at her.

"Dougay, no one has pleased me more than you. Understand that." She reached out her hand to me. I went to shake it, though she had other plans. She dragged me to her bedroom. It was one hell of a way for her to welcome in a lifetime of celibacy.

At Francine's doorway she kissed me farewell. She had on my t-shirt. That kangaroo never looked so good.

Chapter 13

The week dragged by at its normal uneventful pace. The highlight was picking up the signed papers as Francine had organized, Friday at 4pm. On the footpath I looked back at the stone building and up to the windows on the third floor. I wondered if I'd ever be up there again.

Francine had not been there. I hadn't expected her to be, for she was out 'announcing her engagement' somewhere, up there, in the rarefied atmosphere of aspirational society. I walked off wondering what and where that could possibly be. However, my overriding question was not 'what?' or 'where?', rather 'why?'

That evening, after I'd dried the last plate, Claude and I toasted our new-found partnership.

"Here's to your aunt," said Claude.

"My who?" I began, before checking myself.

"May she live a long and fruitful life." He clinked my glass.

"Yes. She wished us both well for the enterprise." One day, I hope to stop telling lies to my friends.

"So, Dougay, any other crazy ideas you have for the place?" he asked, though his heart wasn't in the question.

"Well, Claude, you've got his music playing, so why not a few framed photographs of him hanging on the walls?"

"It's a café, not a gallery."

"Can't it be both?" Sometimes I stumble upon things I have no right thinking. I didn't continue that thought any further as I stopped when photographs of Mozart morphed inside my head into original paintings of him hanging on the walls. I needed time to think about it, for I had awoken in me an idea that I hoped one day would be worth implementing.

"The first thing to do is to expose that arch and then knock out an entrance," I said, beginning to plot and plan. "Sunday week, perhaps you could close the café, and we'll make a start. Your old school friend Remy could dispose of the old bricks and rubble for us in his truck."

On Saturday morning, as I was leaving my apartment building, M'sieur Pom stopped me.

"Look! Dougay, look!" he called, excitedly. He held up the front page of the morning newspaper. "The Mayor's got engaged!" I acted surprised. "It's that woman he's been seen with – remember? She's a lawyer." Francine looked beautiful – of course she did. "He needs a new wife. It's been too long since his first one disappeared."

"Disappeared?"

"Yes, a scandal – ran off with another man – never heard of again. The Mayor was heartbroken."

In the afternoon, I sparred with Remy. After it was over he didn't try anything funny with me.

"You're losing your touch, Remy. No trick, today?"

"No. My thoughts must be elsewhere." We washed our faces and torsos in the large sink in the corner and wiped ourselves down.

"Wish me luck, Dougay," said Remy. "I'm driving up to Eze now."

I made no spoken comment. I only groaned a little while nodding false encouragement. I knew what was up in Eze and I hoped it wasn't too large a dose of disappointment for him.

"Next Sunday, I need a favour from you," I said. "I'll need you to get rid of rubble for me. I'm now a partner with Claude in *L'Opera Mozart* and I'll be knocking in a doorway to connect two rooms." I headed to the door and turned back to him. "Good luck in Eze!"

*

I spent each morning of the following week preparing the walls in the back room, though not the common wall, as that would be prepared once I'd knocked out the archway. I filled the holes and sanded the bumps, painting a sealing coat on several sections which were in need of one. Each night I washed and dried the café's cutlery and swept its floors. It's a very interesting feeling I was now experiencing. The work I was doing in the kitchen hadn't changed, rather it simply felt much more enjoyable knowing the work was for an enterprise which was now partly mine.

I'd been coming from home to the café and then back home again, so I hadn't bumped into Audric and besides I was unable to visit him as I certainly had my hands full. Then Friday afternoon my mobile rang.

"Hi! It's me!" It was the excited voice of Mary-Anne Walton. I dropped my cleaning cloth and wiped my hands on my old jeans. "Guess where I am?" she teased.

"I've no idea," I joyfully answered.

"Cannes."

"What are you doing in Cannes?" I asked, excitement growing in my voice.

"A whirlwind visit – I have to get some signatures on some agreements. You know, investors wanting to be part of Kempenski's next production. Are you free Saturday night?"

"For you, of course." I had been planning on going to *Vlatava-Elbe* and catching up with Milovic, though I'd much prefer the delights of Mary-Anne to those of my Czech mate.

"Saturday night – may I stay at your place?" she asked. "Is that okay?"

"Is that okay?" I asked, not believing my good luck. "Of course – to both questions!"

"Don't shelve your plans. Go wherever you are going; do whatever you are doing; and I'll call you – because I don't know what time I'll be free. I'll get a cab to wherever you are. Okay?"

"Okay. Where have you been staying?" I asked. I was not concerned about that. I just wanted to hear her voice for a while longer.

"On *The Blue Dahlia*. I'd like to see your apartment, particularly the new bathroom."

"The bathroom is gorgeous!" It should be, for Mary-Anne had bought me the maroon border tiles circling the room, contrasting the large light grey wall tiles with their splashes of dark streaks.

"Gotta go! Bye!" And then she added something in English, in her broadest New Jersey accent and laughed, for she knew I didn't understand her.

For the next hour I couldn't concentrate on the job at hand. To take my mind off her, and the upcoming pleasure of tomorrow night, I went to the sink and began washing up.

"You're starting an hour early," commented Claude. "The overtime will have to come out of your five per cent."

*

Saturday morning, I went back to the cafe and finished the dressing of the back room's three walls. Around midday I finished sweeping up.

Saturday afternoon I sparred with Remy. I was leaving, when he spoke. "Friends usually enquire about their mates."

"Enquire about what?" And then I realised. "So – how was Eze?" I asked. Then deliberately I enquired, "How was An-gel-ie?"

"I spent the night." I didn't say anything, for I suspected he hadn't. "On her lounge," he added. I waited for his explanation. I didn't have to wait long. "I was too drunk to drive and there was a thick fog up there. So, we spent the evening sitting by the fire. I've never spoken to a woman like her before."

"It isn't only about speaking, Remy. If you want it to last, you're going to have to listen as well."

"What are you – a free public psychiatrist?"

"Sorry, just trying to help," I said, leaving. I was stopped by Remy's voice.

"As she tossed a blanket over me, I asked her the question."

He had my attention now. "What? The one about having a relationship with her?"

"Yes."

"And?"

"She laughed."

"I told you," I said gently, hoping not to inflict more pain upon him.

"No! She laughed and said, on one condition."

He had me truly hooked now. I closed the steel door behind myself, stepping back into the warehouse, waiting for all the details.

"She wants me to teach her to box – properly. Not that gym punching. She wants to learn the correct stance; how to dance; and to throw a punch correctly. She wants to keep fit, but not by pumping iron. She wants her body to remain ladylike."

Ladylike? I thought, *Throwing punches?* I put my hand on his shoulder. "Remy, most men struggle to find something in common to *talk* about with women. And you're telling me that you and Angelie are planning on *hitting* each other?"

"Yes. I'll take the large punching bag up to her place so she can practise. You and I don't need it."

I didn't know if Remy was stringing me along or not, so I simply said, "That all sounds fine. I've got to go." I left him to his fantasies and headed off towards the night, which hopefully held mine.

*

Milovic and Ulna and Ljuba and Pasha were already lubricated by the time I got there. "Hey!" the collective cry went up.

Milovic shouted, "Milos! Slivovitz!"

"Have you eaten?" I asked Milovic in English.

"No, we were waiting for you."

Milos brought the drinks and I asked, "What's on the menu?"

"No menu tonight – only beef stew and dumplings."

"Okay – I'll have the beef stew and dumplings." Thank goodness they'd all been drinking, for they laughed at my lame gag.

Sometime after a few more beers and slivovitz, Milovic said to me, "Your mobile's ringing."

I hadn't heard it. It was Mary-Anne – ready to join me. I gave her the address and when the cab pulled up in front and she climbed out, Milovic whispered, "I remember her! I drove her to the airport!" Then he leant in to me. "The morning after you'd…"

"Shh!" I hissed.

I couldn't take my eyes from Mary-Anne. She was not in her production assistant mode. Her hair was out and her red ski jacket over her blue jeans splashed colour like a warning beacon out at sea. I was warned and I wasn't looking out for the rocks! I couldn't believe that she was really once more, here, on the Cote d'Azur, with me.

Pasha stood and took her suitcase from the taxi's trunk, as I hadn't moved. I was still sitting, unable to think clearly. She smiled broadly and walked to me. I rose and put out my arms and hugged her as if I never wanted to let her go. We eventually broke from our kiss and I introduced her to everyone. Milovic ordered her a beer, and the evening progressed as if she'd been born and bred in Prague.

I'd forgotten the effect she had on me. I fell silent among my Czech friends. Milovic asked her questions in English and translated her answers for his family. Milos asked for a photograph with her. Ljuba took it on his mobile. I could have stayed like this, watching her forever, as if in the audience of her Royal Command Performance.

A darkened figure walked quickly by us and began to run. Mary-Anne called out, "My case!"

I was off like a shot, running after the grab-and-run thief. I heard a shout behind me and Milovic and Pasha were running as well, though they had crossed to the other side of the street. Twenty metres on the thief realised the suitcase was impeding his progress. He let go of his grip and kept running. I stopped and took hold of the bag and began to drag it back to Mary-Anne.

There was a loud shout further down the street. Milovic and Pasha had the thief between them and were dragging him back to the bar. They flung him down onto the seat in front of Mary-Anne and me.

"Apologise!" Pasha lifted the hood covering the thief's head. He revealed a young woman's face. We all were taken aback.

"I was going to slap *him* around," said Milovic.

"I was going to teach *him* a lesson," added Pasha.

I studied her face. She could have been anywhere between sixteen and twenty-five. It was hard to tell. She had sandy blonde hair and her blue eyes were wide and frightened. Looking furtively about the table, I could have sworn her eyes showed a flicker of recognition when she sighted Mary-Anne. However, I could tell Mary-Anne had no idea who the urchin was.

Sometimes I make a correct decision. I don't know why or where it comes from, I just do. I asked the urchin, "Are you hungry?"

She looked at me as if she didn't understand the question. What she didn't understand was that a victim of her theft could be offering her anything besides a beating.

"Are you hungry?" I asked again.

The others had now realised what I was offering her. They also couldn't believe my question nor why I should ask it.

The young woman nodded.

"The owner only has beef stew and dumplings, so your choice is limited," I explained good naturedly.

The tension at the table eased. She stood as if to leave, though Pasha, still standing behind her, placed a hand on her shoulder.

"No. Don't run," I said, trying to calm her fears. "Sit and Eat. Are you old enough to drink?" She nodded. "Wine? Beer?"

"What's that shit?" she enquired suspiciously, pointing to a shot glass of slivovitz.

"No," I said. "You need to apply to the Czech Embassy for a licence to drink that."

Milos brought the food and she ate. While she did, our conversations returned once more as if she was no longer there, though Pasha kept an eye on her. Mary-Anne kept her hand on her bag.

After a time I asked, "What's your name?" The young woman did not reply. "It's not a trick question," I said. "What do we call you?"

She studied me, and glanced briefly once again at Mary-Anne. She then admitted, "Louise."

When she put down her fork, her plate empty, I asked her, "Do you want a job?"

Mary-Anne looked at me. "Who are you to offer employment to her – or to anyone?"

"Me?" I big noted myself. "I'm a cafe owner!" Mary-Anne did not believe me. My Czech friends did not believe me either.

"Milos!" I called out back towards the bar. "Can I have a pen and paper, please?"

I wrote down my name, my number and the address of *L'Opera Mozart*. I passed the note across the table to Louise.

"I need a waitress. Can you smile?" She forced one. "We'll work on that. Drop in Monday between four and six. The other owner is Claude. I'll be in the kitchen." I didn't say I'd be doing the dishes, as I hoped she'd think I was a chef and therefore the offer would carry more weight.

She stood to go and thanked everyone. Underneath that street urchin facade, she was surprisingly well spoken, with a polite manner. Then she lunged at Pasha's glass of slivovitz, tossing it down her throat. She ran off.

*

I walked Mary-Anne back to my place, dragging her suitcase behind me. On the way she simply informed me, "Dougay, you are a kind-hearted man. However, I fear your unguarded kindness, one day, could get you into trouble."

M'sieur Pom was not at his desk and there was no light from under the door of Madame Legrande's apartment. It was too late for both of them. I was thankful I'd not be wasting time in the foyer introducing Mary-Anne. The gossip would have to wait until the morning when I'd be trying to smuggle her out of the building.

"What a cute old elevator," Mary-Anne whispered, as we rode it up the six flights.

I opened the door to my apartment and dragged in Mary-Anne's suitcase. As I closed the door behind us, Mary Anne pushed me against it, banging my head.

"Ow!" I complained.

"Let me kiss that better for you." She did, her tongue exploring my mouth. I guess she was attempting to heal the back of my head from within.

I don't know how she did it. With her lips never leaving mine, and the back of my head never leaving the door, she managed to unbutton my shirt, pull it open and slide it off. She undid the belt on my trousers and slid them down where they fell over my shoes. Mary Anne was not intending to dance with me! Running her fingers over me from the chest down, she mumbled out of the left hand side of her mouth, "Mmm. You don't need chemicals, do you!"

I mumbled back, "Who needs Viagra when one has you?"

She mumbled out of the other side of her mouth, "You say the sweetest things."

Again, I don't know how she managed it, for she undid her jeans and guided me through the ten basic steps of love making. I'm sure we skipped steps three to eight.

*

Sometime during the night I was kissing Mary-Anne when I rolled over and began kissing Francine. I heard Remy say to me, "Two women? And you're critical of me wanting to be friends with Angelie!" I woke and the room was dark. I lay there listening to the rhythmic breathing of Mary-Anne. I thought of Francine's desire to keep moving up the social ladder and my lack of it. I silently confessed to Francine that I was happy right here, just the way I was.

In the morning Mary-Anne told me that she loved my bathroom renovation, particularly the maroon tiles, which she made an obvious point of reminding me she'd purchased. She also knocked the wind out of my sails when she said that she was flying back to New York, about noon.

*

Before I put her into a cab downstairs, we'd spent the morning talking.

I told her of the plans I had for the apartment; of being a five percent stake holder in the café; and I thanked her, lovingly, physically, for the gift of the maroon tiles.

I walked her to *L'Opera Mozart* and explained that here was the café I was now a proud part owner of. I offered to buy her a croissant and coffee. She insisted on paying, as she said that I was going to need every paying customer I could, now that I was a struggling entrepreneur.

She spoke of the work she was doing for Harold Kempinski, resurrecting a project which went cold five years back. It was a two picture update of the old classic children's story, *Heidi*. Mary-Anne said that it had originally been published in two parts, and Kempenski's idea was to do the exact same thing, to make two movies. They were planning on filming it in Switzerland. She hoped I could join her there during the proposed filming.

She also mentioned the high expectations they all had for *Au Revoir, Mate!* and what the tragic and untimely death of Calvin de Marko would have upon its publicity.

What with my Milan weekend and her star's death, I guess I was going to have to live with keeping a few secrets from her for a while longer.

I didn't want Mary-Anne to catch her flight. I'd have been a very happy man if she suddenly turned to me and said, "Darling, I'm tossing in all that and I want to live with you in a converted studio, without a sea view, and eat stale croissants and cake every day until the café makes a profit."

*

I spent the remainder of Sunday finding the archway and once I had ascertained it had a keystone, knocking out the bricks and plaster and mortar. Remy arrived with his truck. He helped me sweep up all the rubble and dust, and that night we revisited the places where we'd dumped my bathroom rubble.

"She can throw a mean left," he said.

"Angelie?"

"Who else? And she can dance."

"Most women can," I spat out, groaning, as I tossed away a heavy lump of brick and plaster.

"Boxing dance – she's light on her feet – unlike you."

I stood up straight, stretching my back, and looked at him. "Are you going to help me or not?"

"It's your rubble," he simply said.

I bent and threw away more of the building waste. Remy laughed and began to help. After we'd emptied his truck, I said, "Ah, but there's a difference."

"Between what?"

"Between Angelie and me."

"What's that?" asked Remy.

"I'd let you take me to bed!"

Remy looked askance. I stepped into him and kissed him. He suddenly pulled back, spitting out dust and bits of plaster.

*

On Monday between four and six, Louise did not turn up at the café. "Ah, well," I said to myself. "You can only make the offer to help. It's up to them to accept it, or not." I finished and locked up.

I turned the corner for home and stopped. In front, coming towards me was Marcel. "I'd recognize those swinging hips anywhere," I said out loud to myself. Then raising my voice, I called, "The darkness can't hide all the scum in Nice." I hoped he'd heard.

He now saw me and started to sneer, not bothering to hide his contempt.

"On the prowl, Marcel? Hoping to pick up a bit of gutter trade?"

From behind, a cloth was rammed over my nose and mouth. Foolishly, I kept breathing. The last thing I remember was being manhandled into the rear seat of a car.

Chapter 14

I awoke. I was on my back and had difficulty opening my eyes. I managed to squint. There was black above me with pin pricks of light. What kind of room was this? I began to imagine a disco, though there was no spinning ball, only my spinning head. The pin pricks of light were stars. I was outdoors, with a slight weight on my chest.

I began to feel a sharp constant sting in my lower spine. I rolled a little, groaning. Moving my arm elicited the same response. I struggled to feel down there and I eventually took hold of a sharp stone. I flicked it from under me. I collapsed back. I was cold. I glanced down at my chest. The weight was my wallet and mobile. *What thoughtful assholes*, I consoled myself.

I was naked – no wonder I was cold. I tried to move to get up. I couldn't. There was nothing holding me down, nothing tied around my limbs, however I just couldn't move without an enormous amount of pain shooting through me. That's the thing about pain, it hurts.

Where was I? I couldn't turn my head too far to either side. My limbs weren't working. My eyesight was working, though partially, as my eye lids felt pulled together. My nose felt damaged, though I could still smell with it and where I was smelt like a garbage tip. I remembered the final resting place of Danielle Hubert. My mind still had its senses and I thought, *a garbage dump – how ironic*.

I lay for a while wondering how I was going to manage to get up – which side I'd roll onto and which arm I'd use to push with. There was something up my ass.

I groaned as I reached down there and managed to withdraw a sachet of white powder. "Oh no!" My voice was still working, though croakily. It was time to move. I couldn't be found like this – being naked didn't worry me, rather I didn't want to be found with a sachet of cocaine up my ass! I groaned, exerting myself, pitching the shit stained sachet into the tip.

I rolled and struggled onto all fours. I gently brushed some dirt off my arms and stomach. My groin throbbed. There was no woman I knew who was planning on having my children, so I accepted that the pain would eventually leave me, though the damage may not.

Over to my left were my trousers. I looked the other way. My underwear was over to my right. I crawled that way. I stopped halfway because my knees were digging into gravel. I had to get up. With everything I could muster, I stood and swayed and very nearly fell back down. I danced a little to stay upright, the soles of my feet digging into more of the sharp stones.

I pulled on my underpants with one arm. I pulled my T-shirt over my head, using the same arm, and bent my neck and used part of my mouth to tug it. I stumbled over to my trousers and leaning down, opened them and shook the legs free of the ball they'd been wrapped up in. I put in my wallet and mobile, then left leg, followed by right.

I couldn't search for my shirt as I had to gather myself once more. I breathed in deeply. My ribs hurt. I decided to take shallow breaths, merely topping up the supply I needed.

My slit eyes had adjusted to the dark. Perhaps there was a moon over head, for the area was now washed in dull silver. My shirt was further on from my trousers. I stumbled there and managed to fling it about my shoulders and get my right arm in. My left arm was still most uncooperative.

Where was my goatskin jacket? "They haven't made a souvenir of my jacket have they?" I wondered out loud. No, it was still further over, carefully arranged on top of rotting vegetables. When I got to it, I peeled off a deliberately placed large, soft and squashy zucchini.

I couldn't find my shoes. I tip-toed on further – they weren't there. I turned back to where I'd been dumped. I could make out something that resembled a shoe in the distance. My assailants had a sense of humour! I made my way back to it. Both shoes were lying, waiting for me, a sock in each. I managed to get the left combination on while standing, however I toppled over once I started to attempt the right. Completed, I sat in the dirt and with a huge effort lifted myself to my feet.

I was now, finally, the best dressed man in the garbage dump tonight.

I didn't know which way to walk to leave it. Off to my right lay a dirt track that vehicles used. It was more a gravel laneway and I began to realize that the garbage dump was not an official one, rather a make shift one that locals dumped their stuff in to avoid paying fees. I looked about. Which direction to walk? Whichever way I chose, it was sure to be the wrong one.

I moved on a little way from the worst of the smell. I still had my watch on my left wrist. They'd not robbed me of a thing. They'd beaten me – and of course, they'd humiliated me. Humiliation. That's what I'd made Marcel feel when he had to apologise to Claude, face to face. Yes, now I understood everything. This was retribution for Marcel's humiliation and for the beating that M. Beret and M. Baldy had been handed out in that lane outside the *D'Accord Café*.

My watch read 4.17 am. I was suddenly cold again. I wrapped my arms around myself and pulled up my scarf. Where was my scarf? In the dull silver light I looked about. I searched the area where my clothing had been scattered. They had taken one thing – the scarf Madame Legrande had knitted and presented me a few weeks back. How was I ever going to explain its disappearance?

Over from me and behind, I heard a truck change gears. There was a road over there. I staggered to it.

Ahead of me I could see the occasional early morning vehicle pass in either direction. I still didn't know which way Nice city centre lay. I took out my mobile to see where I really was. Tapping on 'my location', I stared in disbelief. I was on the outskirts of Aix-en-Provence!

*

As dawn came, a police car slowed and stopped in front of me. "Any chance of a lift to Nice?" I asked through an aching jaw. Police, the world over, are not known for their appreciation of wit. They certainly do not possess repartee, for these two spread my legs against the bonnet of their car and frisked me. They studied my wallet, in particular my identification. "I believe there's about fifty five euro in there," I said out the left side of my swollen lips. "I expect it to be there when my wallet's returned."

The large policeman placed it back in my trousers and sealed the delivery with a jab to the kidneys. As luck would have it, he managed to find the one spot on my entire body which hadn't already been thumped. I fell to my knees beside the car. To a passer-by it appeared as if I was saying a prayer to the God of Law and Order.

They hauled me up and one of them undid my belt, then the other from behind slid down my pants and began digging into my ass! I wriggled. "What you think you're doing?" I asked, shocked. "We haven't been properly introduced yet!"

"Nothing," one of them said. He didn't say it to me – he said it to his partner. Nothing? He'd found nothing? They'd been searching for the cachet of coke! Someone had tipped them off.

They waved down a passing motorist. Tossing me onto the back seat of her car, they ordered the surprised lady, "Take him to the train station."

"But he's all dirty," she protested.

"You've got a faulty tail light," one of the brainless cops said.

"No, I haven't," she replied, indignant that anything on her car would be less than perfect.

"If you don't take him there, you soon will have." The two uniformed 'brain surgeons' guffawed.

She drove off and I thanked her as I fell out of her car at the station. I don't know what she looked like, for my left eye was now sealed and the swelling was starting to move downwards and join up with the swelling rising from my cheek.

I rummaged through my wallet at the ticket office. I handed something to the seller and said, "One way to Marseille, please. Will this do?" She looked at it puzzled. It was an old rewards card from a supermarket on Bondi Beach.

"Keep it, it's yours," I said. "They have a special on chicken wings this week."

I bought the cheapest ticket. She handed me the change, hoping I'd move on and count it someplace else.

A little after 8am, I staggered on board a train and sometime later in Marseille, I had a ticket for Nice and was waiting on the correct platform.

A hand was shaking me, and a young voice was saying, "Monsieur. Monsieur – the train – it's leaving." I smiled a thank you and raised my face towards him. The kid took one look at my contorted mouth beneath my blackening swollen eyes and ran off to his mother. I followed and the three of us jumped into the carriage. That exertion hurt – really hurt. I sat clutching my ribs and my guts.

I took the train to Nice.

Another hand was shaking me. "Monsieur, monsieur." It was an older male voice. It was the conductor. "Get off. Get off." He helped me up and escorted me from the train. *Such kindness*, I thought. Where was I? The platform was dark – underground. I had slept beyond Nice and was now in Monaco.

I dragged myself up the huge staircase, found the ticket seller and bought another ticket back to Nice.

The train lurched to a stop at Villefranche-sur-mer, waking me. While some passengers got on board, I again remembered that wonderful Sunday afternoon spent with Francine, amongst the happy families and lovers and screaming children. A few days later I'd told her I loved her. Did that experience influence me? Is that what I was missing in my life? Family? I wished Francine was with me right now. Or was that Mary-Anne? Either one – I'd curl up in her arms and ask her to take care of me. However, Mary-Anne had flown back to New York and the world of movie production and Francine had gone off to marry her gay society pass.

If I lived to see the summer, I decided I'd bring Mary-Anne here, to Villefranche-sur-mer. Though to tell the truth, I'd love another trip on *The Blue Dahlia*, Kempenski's yacht, to that unnamed beach near the Italian border with her – lying in the sand, frolicking in the water. I couldn't afford to dream of that, so I stood and held onto the pole, in the centre of the carriage. It's difficult for me to fall asleep standing.

*

I raised my right hand in a half-hearted greeting to M'sieur Pom as I staggered across the foyer of my apartment's building. By the time I'd managed the few steps to the elevator he was beside me holding me by the arm. He wrestled with the iron doors and escorted me up.

"My key is in my wallet," I managed to say out the corner of my twisted mouth. He opened the door and led me in, carefully sitting me on my bed, removing my shoes. I fell back, relieved.

Home – at last, home. You could lay me down on the best bed in Versailles and it would be nothing like the feeling I was now experiencing. My bed. My apartment. My home.

Chapter 15

When I awoke, Madame Legrande was removing my socks.

"Lift your shoulders a little," she said. I did and she delicately slid my shirt around me and over my head. She lifted the sleeves off my aching half extended arms. She took hold of my t-shirt and repeated the action. "Okay, lift your bottom," she requested.

"Madame, you're not going to take off my trousers, are you?"

"All your clothing has to be washed. You stink." I couldn't disagree with that. "I have never smelt such smells on a living human being before." She gently prodded me to lift my buttocks. "I'm a widow and I've raised two sons. So, nothing you own is going to worry me one iota." In one movement she whipped my trousers and underpants down. "Well, the ladies of Nice are not going to get too excited about that!" She laughed and laughed and laughed.

What is it about my friends? Why do they think, even in my most vulnerable state, that I'm a figure of fun?

She gathered my clothing, bundled it into a plastic laundry bag and dumped it out of the way by the door. She was planning on taking it and washing it for me. I didn't mind my friends making fun of me after all.

"I'm getting cold here," I complained.

"Men! You make the worst patients."

She returned from the bathroom and placed a warm washer on my chest and began to gently wash and dry the front of me from head to toe. "Roll over on your side," she ordered.

"Which one?"

She tickled me on my right. I rolled that way. She continued washing and drying me. Somehow, I lay on my stomach and she completed my bath.

"I'm sorry to put you through this," I said.

"No matter."

"It can't be pleasant for you."

"It's not too bad. I'm imagining you're Yves Montand."

I nodded off, her laughter not seeming to stop.

*

"I need a leak, Madame." I tried to get up – I couldn't. My limbs didn't want to work. My head fell back on the pillow. Madame Legrande found an old saucepan under my kitchen sink.

"Roll on your side," she said.

I struggled to do so. She held me by my shoulders until I was propped there. She eased down the shorts she'd dressed me in. I didn't complain. Like a baby, I urinated into the tin pot.

As she took it into the bathroom to empty, I managed to call out, "I won't be having coffee!" I tried to laugh – I could only manage a painful, side splitting cough.

"Leave the jokes to me!" she called back. "You and your humour are sick!"

*

I woke with a cold thing on my chest. It was a stethoscope and a moustachioed gentleman in a suit was leaning over me.

"I can't afford a doctor," I said to whoever was listening.

I heard Madame's voice. "I'm a rich old lady and I'll spend my money on whatever I choose to. Now stop complaining. If all Australians are like you, then Heaven help the Southern Hemisphere."

"I'm French. I was born …" A thermometer was shoved into my mouth.

The doctor rolled me over onto my side and sent a chill down my spine when he placed the stethoscope on my back, saying, "Breathe deeply, Monsieur, breathe deeply." Why do doctors never warm their stethoscopes?

*

"Plenty of rest. The facial swelling will go down before the week is out." I heard the door shut.

Madame Legrande came into the bedroom. She saw I'd woken again. "The doctor says you're going to need an X-ray. Though your face will only be saved by extensive plastic surgery. He thinks he can save all the ugly bits as well." She laughed and laughed.

"An X-ray? I don't have Hospital Cover."

"We have ways …"

*

I was propped in the elevator and heading down to the foyer. On one side of me was M'sieur Pom and on the other – Detective Legrande! I wasn't being arrested, was I? They led me out to a parked car. They tried to seat me in the back, however I resisted.

"No. Better if I lie down," I managed to say. They gently slid me in on my stomach.

Outside the hospital, Raphael was dragging me out and had me on my feet, when a hospital parking official said, "You can't park here."

Raphael showed him his badge, and said, "Keep watch on this car. Don't let anyone move it. There is valuable DNA inside."

"Yes, sir," said the officious attendant.

With my arm over his shoulder, Raphael led me carefully inside. There he asked at reception, "Is Doctor Constance Armand on duty, nurse?"

"Yes sir."

"Call her please."

"Sir, I just can't …"

Raphael showed his badge, explaining to the triage nurse, "This man is a suspect in an international conspiracy. I need him X-rayed to see if he's fit to be deported to Australia."

Doctor Armand appeared and escorted us through a series of doors. Inside, she said to the attendant, "X-ray his chest. All over, please." I was placed against a machine. My bones were filmed. I was turned ninety degrees and made to hold my arms above my head. "Elbows to ear level will suffice," I heard her say. I struggled to hold them there. I was filmed again.

She put my shirt back on and Raphael once again maneuvered me to his waiting car. When we were leaving the X-ray suite, I'm sure I heard her say to him, "What time are you picking me up this evening?"

*

I awoke and thought I'd died. Claude was leaning over me. "Ah – you're alive," he joked.

"I'm sorry, Claude. I've let you down. I haven't been able to wash and sweep for you. I've been detained."

"It's okay, Mon Ami." Claude dismissed my concern, patting the fingers of my interlocked hands on my chest.

"I still have the painting of the new room to do," I remembered.

"It's okay – get well – don't worry about your job. That girl you hired, she turned up on Tuesday."

"What girl?"

"Louise."

"Louise? I don't know any … Oh, yes. Did she?"

"I didn't believe her at first, until she showed me the note you'd written her. I recognized your hand writing."

"I can't write French."

"Maybe not, but you can write French numbers."

*

Madame Legrande was fussing about me, tucking in my bed clothes. "Nice pink duvet," she said. "The doctor called to say he's received your X-rays. Nothing's cracked, though your ribs are heavily bruised. All your muscles are inflamed, so he's prescribed these for you. Open your mouth."

I resisted. "Madame, who paid for these?" I was not happy with her generosity, though I was grateful.

"No questions – open your mouth."

Madame Legrande held out a small collection of different coloured drugs. I did as asked and she popped the pills and tablets in and spilt water down my throat as I tried to drink. She wiped my chin.

"You are as clumsy as a baby," she gently admonished.

"Madame, I was not the one pouring the water!"

"Oh," she said concerned.

"What is it?"

"I've just read the label. I've given you three, not one tablet."

"What are they?" I asked, concerned.

"Sleeping pills."

*

Remy called by and asked if I wanted a friendly spar. I was only half awake, so I didn't know if he meant with him or Angelie.

M'sieur Pom was with him and another man, Remy called Electro. They carried into my living room a large screen television!

I managed to utter, "Where'd that come from?" Before Remy could reply, I added, "Off the back of a truck!" All three laughed.

They fiddled out there for over an hour. I laid back, my eyes on the ceiling, listening as Remy and M'sieur Pom debated about where to place it to get the best angle for the maximum viewing effect in the small area. Then Electro went to work and after a lot of drilling and grunting, somehow managed to wire the thing up. Remy told me that he'd also managed to find a DVD player. He made some lame joke about me not knowing what it was, as we probably didn't have them back in Australia! After they turned the television on and tuned everything to perfection, Remy said I owed Electro a night on the slivovitz – for 'services rendered'!

*

I woke to the sound of snoring, coming from beside me on my bed. Someone was stretched out on top of the pink duvet. I was on my side and looking towards the window. The quality of light out there made me think it was afternoon. I noted Madame Legrande's coat on the back of the bedside chair.

I hoped she was dreaming of Jean Paul Belmondo. I hoped one day a lover would take as much care of me as she had been doing. I hoped Mary-Anne would be back for the summer.

Chapter 16

I was sitting with Madame Legrande on our favourite bench in Place Mozart. There was an hour of late autumn sun and we were taking advantage of it. From across Rue Beethoven, Raphael walked to us.

"Thank you, for the X-rays," I said, smiling.

"That's okay." After kissing his mother, he sat, placing me between himself and her.

"Do you know," I began, "your calculations do not hold water." He looked at me, not understanding. "That disappearing baby could not be your case, as forty years ago you'd have only been thirteen or fourteen." His mother was curious now. "Your sons love a smoke screen, Madame."

"Ah, that genetic trait comes from their father, I'm afraid. He could only come to the point via a circuitous route."

"Okay, okay," said Raphael. "I'll come to the point." He cleared his throat. "You remember, Detective LaCrosse, Maman?"

"Yes. He'd be retired by now, wouldn't he?" she asked.

"Several years ago. Cancer. Sadly, he died recently."

"Oh, that's a shame." She automatically blessed herself. "Give my regards to his widow," she added, genuinely concerned.

To me, Raphael said, "I've been trying to tie up in a neat little bow, for him, the thing that seemed to bug him forever. You see, he worked the case. I confess, I was impressed with how you stumbled upon the solution to Danielle's death and I thought you might find a thread out there, somewhere, which could ease the concern for a decent, old detective, who was my mentor. I've always kept out an eye and an ear for him, hoping to see a clue or hear a careless word about the disappearance. I've never managed to come across anything and so I just wondered if you could. Like him, I've been puzzled by it as well."

"Most lives end with threads *not* tied up in a neat bow," I said.

He looked at me. "What are you – a part time philosopher?"

Madame Legrande laughed. "No, Raphael. What he is – is no threat to the ladies!" She laughed at her own joke.

"Pay no concern to my mother," said Raphael. "She laughed at her sons growing up as well. Take it as a compliment."

"He knows, he knows," she said, patting my knee.

"So," Raphael asked in his detective voice, "who beat the shit out of you?"

"I don't know." He didn't say anything. "Truly. I could not select him, or them, in an identity parade."

"But – you have your suspicions." I didn't say a thing. He kissed his mother goodbye and began to walk off.

"That's it?" I called after him. "That's what you dropped by to say?"

He came back to me. "There are constant changes in the criminal landscape of Nice. My job is not only to solve crime but also to be aware of any new possible source of it. I thought perhaps you'd put your finger into a pie you had no right to taste. The bashing you received was hardly a love pat. Someone wanted you hurt and to be taught a lesson."

He waited a moment to let that sink in.

"And the person, or persons, who administered it, knew exactly what they were doing. Why do you think you're still alive? They weren't amateurs." He studied me with concern. "Look after yourself, Dougay."

*

Several days later I felt well enough to pick up a cloth and begin work on the walls in the back room at *L'Opera Mozart*. I glanced up and studied the state of the ceiling – dirty, not damaged – and felt no desire to clean it. I did not wish to stand below it, holding onto a long pole, my arms above my head. I gave up.

I called Audric, not that I wanted to go on a long walk with him. I just wanted to see how he was getting on. It had been quite a while since we last spoke. He invited me over.

Audric had an espresso machine and I didn't refuse a cup. While he was making it, I looked at the three photographs on the mantelpiece over the fireplace, which had been boarded up. There was a portrait of his wife. He hadn't lied to me. She had been a very beautiful woman – vibrant eyes, with a smile to die for, her face surrounded by short cropped black hair. Their wedding photograph was a study in joyousness. The third photograph was of them, with a babe in Audric's arms. The adults were kneeling and the photograph seemed to be taken where I was now standing. A fire was burning in the grill behind them.

I began to feel a little regret, for most people had a baby photograph of their child, though my parents never did. It was for protection – nothing to link them to a life back here in France.

"My wife was extremely beautiful, was she not?" said Audric, passing me a hot coffee mug.

"Yes – very. And your child? How old is he or she now?"

"Sadly – he died not long after that photograph." I glanced again at it. I now noted his wife was not smiling as carefree as she was on her wedding day. Motherhood can be a rude awakening, I guess.

"I'm sorry," I said, "I didn't mean to pry."

We sat and sipped our coffee. "Good coffee," I commented. Audric didn't hear me, as he was still away with his memories.

"The loss of our child weighed heavily upon her," he said. "Don't get me wrong. I was devastated as well. Babette seemed to drift away, become enclosed. Over a short period she just seemed to sap the life from me."

He was now returning to the specific thoughts he'd expressed when we'd first began to walk together. I nodded as if I had an understanding of all he was saying.

"I tried everything to ease her concerns or her worries or whatever she was suffering. It was to no avail. She didn't wish to even leave the house. I could not reach her anymore."

I nodded and sipped my coffee.

"Before we wed, we talked of dreams and hopes and – you know – all the things young people discuss on the verge of marriage."

He stood and went to the wedding photograph. He picked it up and carried it to me. "Look at her eyes. Have you ever seen such happiness, such belief in the future?" I hadn't.

"Who's the man in the background?" I asked.

"Oh, that's Xebec, her brother. He's a painter, an artist. That's tragic as well. He's in – 'inside', you know – a hospital. I pay his fees, it's the least I can do for Babette."

Audric returned the photograph and changed the subject. I guess after forty years you grow weary of telling and re-living the same stories.

"What do you do, Dougay?" he asked.

"Oh, odd jobs – this and that. I've recently become a very small shareholder in the café where I occasionally work."

"Yes, you've told me. It's good to have an investment. It means you have a future."

"I also help out a friend who has a warehouse. He deals in used furniture. He's dodgy but trustworthy."

"Isn't that a contradiction in terms?"

"Yes – and he is a *complete* contradiction."

Audric sat back and settled a little. "I've been thinking of moving," he confessed. "I've always wanted to live in Paris."

"The lure of the bright lights and endless nights of partying are calling you?" I asked cheekily. He smiled, not being tempted by that at all. "What's stopping you?" I asked.

"Well – I pay for Xebec – his upkeep."

"These days, you can pay that over the internet."

"True. It's just…"

"Audric," I dropped my voice, "Forgive me for saying it like this – Babette is not coming back."

He sighed and nodded. "If I decided to sell up here, can your friend come and give me a price on everything?"

"Everything in the house?"

"Yes. There are things he can throw away or burn. Whatever he does with them will not worry me. If I make the break, I want it to be a complete one."

We sat and said nothing further. He was off in his thoughts again. I guess each piece of furniture held a special memory – from where it had been purchased or from what maiden aunt it had been given.

After a while he asked if I'd like another coffee. I said I would and when he went off to make it, I crossed to the mantelpiece again and studied the photographs. Audric returned with the two large cups.

"Your brother-in-law – was he successful before his breakdown?"

"I think so. He had a few commissions – the small churches managed to pay him for some paintings. Though I will say, the reputation of Van Gogh is still intact. He did landscapes of the region; religious settings; various poses of 'Madonna and Child'."

A bell rang somewhere in my head. I recalled Ljuba's birthday party and mention of her artistic inmate, the one who'd been spoken to by God.

Audric returned to his memories. "My wife would simply sit – sit where you're now sitting. I was unable to break through her outer shell. The more I tried, the stronger her resistance. You notice little things at first, don't you?" he asked rhetorically. "Then they gradually increase. Towards the end she'd cradle herself, rocking back and forth, her eyes closed, off in a world only she occupied."

It was time I changed the subject. "I'm renovating my cafe – it's the one I took you to after we visited Babette's grave, remember?"

"Yes, of course – Mozart something."

"*L'Opera Mozart*. Well, I'm going to need some prints or paintings to hang on the walls after I finish preparing them. I wonder if I might be able to buy some from your brother-in-law – if they're suitable. My partner, Claude, will complain about the added cost, but perhaps I can persuade him to purchase one or two – if they're any good. A sale might help your brother – you know, mentally."

"That's very decent of you, Dougay. He might like that. Yes, a boost to his well-being. Come with me when I visit him next week."

*

That evening I returned to work and saw Louise for the first time since I'd 'hired' her. She thanked me for the job. She'd changed. There was a confidence in her that employment brings. Because she was a beautiful young woman, I suggested to Claude that he keep her on. I'd still do the kitchen chores, at a reduced fee, and she could serve the tables and smile at all the customers. He agreed and her presence was to be a marked improvement to the flavour of the cafe. Better a pretty young woman than two grumpy middle-aged men fronting the establishment.

I didn't keep a survey, however after a day or two I said to Claude, "I believe we're getting a more regular customer. People are coming back for a coffee more often."

"Yes – particularly all the dirty old men," he sniggered.

"Does it matter?" I asked. "As long as their euro isn't counterfeit, they're welcome. Besides having young people around helps keep you old folk smiling."

He scoffed back at me. Now was the time to put into his head the idea of purchasing a few paintings for the walls of the back room. "Claude, I've been thinking…"

"No!"

*

"Are we doing anything for Christmas?" I asked. I was sitting with Claude and Louise around a table in the darkened cafe. Louise had stacked the chairs on the tables; Claude had swept out; and I'd put away the last knife.

"Nothing," said Claude. "Louise?"

"Nothing," she replied.

"Nothing?" I queried. I'd made no attempt to question her about the life she led or the life she may have fled, so I was surprised when she said 'nothing' so quickly and so definitively. I didn't push it – what family or friends she had, or didn't have, was none of my business.

"Well then," I went on, "perhaps we could invite some lonely guys and gals to a Christmas lunch. I know a few who may have no place to go."

"I will cook," said Louise. Both Claude and I looked at her, surprised by her eagerness to contribute, to be a part of a hastily arranged event.

"I *can* cook," she said, trying to dispel any doubts she felt we may have had.

"Okay," I said, encouraging her, though really trying to convince Claude. "Roast chicken – and cold ham."

"Cold?" she asked.

"Home in Australia, Christmas food was always dominated by cold ham. In fact, everything was cold. Chicken, pork, prawns."

"Prawns? We can't afford prawns!" complained Claude.

"No prawns," I said, not wanting him to put a dampener on the idea of Christmas lunch before it had even got off the drawing boards.

Louise was making notes on a piece of paper. On closer look they were ingredients she'd needed to buy. "How many people, Dougay?" she asked.

I did a quick head count. "I can think of three or four. I don't know how many for Claude. What about you?"

"None," said Louise.

Claude and I let the finality of her comment linger, slowly exchanging glances with each other.

I should have gone home, however I decided to lash out and have another beer – or two. Louise asked if she could have one. I said she could and that I was paying, for she needed to save her money.

Sometimes I say silly things to women. "Louise, you're very pretty. Ever think of being an actress?" She flinched.

"No – never," she said. I'd touched a nerve. I let the idea drop and sipped my beer.

*

Two days later I went with Audric to Clinique de Cote d'Azur. It is up in the hills, overlooking the city, between Musee National Marc Chagall and Musee Matisse, towards the top end, nearby the Archelogique de Nice.

I followed Audric through the foyer and past a beautifully crafted sweeping wooden staircase. It was well maintained, the bare boards lacquered and polished, bringing out the deep reddish colour of the timber.

Ljuba was on duty out in the gardens at the rear of the building. I gave her a wave and we chatted briefly. Audric pointed to a gentleman sitting under a tree on a two-seater bench, crossing to him. After my brief conversation with Ljuba, I joined him and his brother in law, sitting at their knees on the ground, like an apprentice to Socrates, though I didn't expect too many philosophical words of wisdom from Xebec.

After the introductions, which Xebec failed to register, Audric explained to him that I may be interested in buying one of his paintings.

"A landscape," I qualified, as I didn't want any religious overtones in the cafe. "Or, perhaps, a portrait of Mozart!" Xebec looked at me, puzzled. I explained the name of the cafe, and how it might be a good idea to have a painting of the boy genius.

"A landscape?" I suggested again, trying to help him focus his thoughts as the explanation of Mozart and my cafe had seemed to cast a vacant wash over his face. I felt he understood 'landscape', though he made no comment. He merely turned away and stretched out his feet into the small sliver of sunlight filtering through the overhead tree. Was he thinking of a picturesque scene he could realise? Or thinking of little Wolfgang at the piano? Who could tell? If I could read the thoughts of the insane, I'd be an extremely wealthy person.

Audric tried to engage him in further conversation, though most of his questions weren't answered. My attention was drawn to others sitting out there, rugged up from the chill, content to be there, whether naturally or drug induced. An hour later Audric stood. I followed him from the garden back to the main building.

"Is he always like that?" I asked Audric as we neared the staircase, stepping into the reception area. "He's not very talkative."

"He's always like that – though today he's not painting. I don't come for the answers. I come to – you know – I owe it to Babette."

Ljuba was near the doorway, as we pushed it open. She said, "Au revoir, Monsieur Lefbvre."

Chapter 17

"Au revoir, Madame," said Audric, walking on.

I didn't follow him. "Lefbvre?" I asked Ljuba.

"Yes. Dougay, have you been drinking too much slivovitz?" asked Ljuba, smiling teasingly. "Who did you think your friend is?"

I improvised quickly. "Ljuba, Audric has asked me to visit his brother-in-law on Christmas morning," I lied. "He can't make it. Will you be on duty?"

"Yes. The last nurses hired will be the ones working that day. The others have Christmas at home."

I understood. "I'll see you Christmas morning." I turned to go then stopped. "Ljuba, do I need to sign something to say I'm coming to visit Xebec Paquet?"

"Who?" she asked puzzled. "Dougay, are you making fun of me? He's Xebec Fabron."

I ran several metres, catching up with Audric.

"I know the nurse back there. She called you 'Monsieur Lefbvre'."

"Yes," he replied, unconcerned by my question.

"Your wife's grave read, 'Babette Paquet'."

He stopped walking, turning to me with sadness taking over his eyes. "Towards the end, she insisted on being buried under her maiden name – another stab to the heart." He walked on, I followed.

"And Xebec – he's your brother-in-law, right?"

"Half."

"Half?"

"Yes, his father's name was Fabron. He and Babette had different fathers – same mother. He's the elder."

Something from way back in my brain told me that some forms of mental illness are carried by the mother and appear in their male offspring. Xebec certainly had a mental illness, and Babette's behaviour, towards the end of her life, for whatever reason, suggested she was walking down the same path.

I took Audric by the arm. "Tell me truthfully. Is 'Audric' your real name?"

"Truthfully? Why should I lie? Yes, though technically no."

"What does that mean?"

"'Audric' was the name of my adored grandfather, and my parents called me that from a very young age. It stuck. To everyone I am known as 'Audric'."

"And really you are?"

"Carvell – Carvell Lefbvre."

*

That afternoon I began cleaning the ceiling in the back room of the cafe. I could only manage fifteen or twenty minutes without having to stop and stretch and rub out my aching shoulders. I constantly thought of Audric and what I'd stumbled upon.

Audric had said that his child had died. His saying that could be simply for self-protection, to keep further prying questions at bay. Once a babe is dead no one asks what became of it. People nod their compassionate understanding, and not wishing to inflict more pain, move on. Death is final, abduction is not. According to Detective Raphael Legrande, Carvell Lefbvre's child had disappeared. Could the baby have been kidnapped after all?

I was keen to revisit the half brother-in-law, to see if he could, in some way, throw light on Raphael's puzzle. It wasn't just Raphael's puzzle, it was becoming mine as well. I didn't want to confront Audric directly, not yet anyway, perhaps never, for I really liked the man and all those memories he spasmodically allowed me into were clearly painful ones. When he had spoken of his child, I did not hear a false note in his voice. He wasn't covering up anything.

I called Remy and he dropped by with two step ladders and a plank. Claude went off and bought the white ceiling paint and the cream for the walls. I used a brush to cut in and a roller to spread the paint from the edge of the ceiling towards the centre.

By closing time, I had completed the first coat. Louise brought me a beer. "Who's paying for this?" I asked. "I hope you're not."

"No," she said. "Claude said to put it on *your* tab."

I was too tired to laugh or cry or complain or celebrate. When Claude poked his head in from talking to the last customer, I said, "I'll do the second ceiling coat tomorrow, and hopefully the first coat of the walls. I want it finished before Christmas."

I took home two croissants and a slice of cake. I poured a large glass of water and fell into bed. Sometimes, I'm just too exhausted to go out partying, so I party at home.

*

True to my word, I finished the ceiling and the first coat of the walls. I even helped Louise clean the rarely used kitchen stove. She scrubbed the top into shape and I had the unpleasant task of getting rid of layers of splattered fat from inside the oven. With darkness closing in, I turned on the lights and started the second coat on the walls.

Once Claude locked up, Louise began cooking. She told both of us we were not allowed to look over her shoulder, nor offer advice. After an hour it began to smell invitingly tempting in and around the kitchen. In a funny way it all felt very homely – painting the walls, smelling the roast chicken, listening to Claude attempt to sing some Christmas carols in French. That brought back memories of my mother singing them to me, though she could sing in tune.

I finally slumped back in a chair. I looked up and laughed. While I'd been painting and Louise had been cooking, Claude had found old decorations and strung up rows of frilly green and red tinsel around the main room. He did not have a designer's eye, for they were looped lopsidedly on the walls. When he dropped a beer into my hand I said, "Nice job, Claude – for Christmas at the blind school."

"And a Merry Christmas to you, too, Dougay," he said pointedly.

I raised the bottle in a toast. It was Christmas Eve and I'd forgotten.

Louise put a small platter in front of us – meats, vegetables and the ubiquitous bread stick. "A preview of tomorrow," she said. She handed out cutlery and plates and we wolfed in.

"Wow! Louise, I never knew you were such a good cook." I meant it. She'd added some spices to the chicken and whatever the accompanying sauce was, it was delicious. "Claude," I started.

"No!"

"Claude," I reiterated.

"I'll think about it."

*

In the elevator on the way down, I opened the iron door for Monsieur Degas. I wished him a cheery, "Merry Christmas, Monsieur!"

"Merci, Dougay," he replied. I felt he was pleased to have received the greeting.

"Are you having lunch with family?" I wondered, as I knew nothing of his life.

"Yes, with a daughter and a son and their families," he said, though I got the impression that he wasn't too keen on going. "I take a bus to my daughter's apartment and they bring me home about 5pm."

I let him out into the foyer and he walked off out of the building, not stopping as M'sieur Pom was not at his desk.

I knocked on the apartment door of Madame Legrande. She opened it and before she could welcome me, I handed her a box of chocolates, kissed her on the cheek and wished her, "*Joyeux Noel*!" I walked off.

She called after me, "You're a naughty boy, Dougay. You shouldn't have. Wait!" I stopped and walked back to her apartment. She was standing a step inside, grinning with her hands behind her back. She brought them around and presented me with a scarf, a replica of the one she'd knitted, the one I'd had stolen from me at that garbage dump outside of Aix-en-Provence.

"Another scarf?"

"Yes. I'm intending to leave you twice!" We laughed. She tied the grey and red scarf carefully around my neck. She stepped back and looked at me. "You'll do," she said and patted me on the arm.

"Madame, try and make it to *L'Opera Mozart* this afternoon or evening."

"I'll do my best, though remember, I have two sons and their ego pulls me both ways on Christmas day." I understood.

M'sieur Pom appeared in the foyer from his apartment. "Keep the noise down you two. It's Christmas!" he shouted.

I went to him and gave him the other box of chocolates. "It's for your wife, not you," I stipulated.

From under his desk, he poured me a glass of schnapps. "Merry Christmas, Dougay!"

"Merry Christmas, M'sieur Pom!" We knocked back the schnapps. "Drop in to the cafe whenever you can. And bring your wife," I insisted.

From inside their apartment, off the foyer, I heard her call out, "I'll be there! With or without the old guard dog!"

*

Ljuba was at the front desk of the clinic, dwarfed by the staircase above.

"Nice scarf," she commented.

"Thank you, it's a Christmas gift."

"He's out under the tree. Come on." We crossed the foyer and out through the door that led into the garden.

Xebec was sitting on the same bench as before, though this time he had an easel before him and a brush in his hand. A small collapsible table held his paints and cloths and other assorted junk painters require.

I sat beside him. He didn't look at me, as he was fixated on the canvas.

He was forming a painting of 'Madonna and Child', as he'd completed a charcoaled outline. What took my eye and refused to let go of it, was the Madonna's face. It was painted, complete and to perfection. In the surrounding space of the canvas, it was as if her head was suspended in mid-air, strange charcoal lines dangling from the chin and partially realised neck, like one of those large undersea jelly fish.

Xebec was an excellent portrait painter. The short black hair framed the beautiful smile and the glowing bright green eyes. Remembering the photograph on Audric's mantel piece, he'd caught his half-sister, Babette, to perfection.

I settled back onto the bench, saying nothing, watching him work. He began to place some colour on the background – maybe he was in his 'landscape mode' now. I know nothing about painting – the process one goes through. I stared at the painting. It was extremely disconcerting to see the Madonna's face fully realised, staring out at me, hypnotically suspended, with nothing around it or supporting it.

"She's very beautiful," I said.

Xebec said nothing.

"Captivating eyes – beautiful – the woman," I said a little louder.

"Yes," he managed.

"Who is she?" I asked, hoping to start a conversation. Xebec offered no reply. "Xebec, who is she?" I asked a little firmer.

"Sister."

I waited, hoping he'd go on. He muttered something I didn't quite catch. It sounded like 'love'.

I've said before that some things just spring to my mind from out of nowhere.

"Xebec," I said, gently taking his chin in my hand and turning his face towards me, enabling me to look into his eyes, "What's it like to fuck your sister?"

He jumped me.

Screaming in an explosive rage, he fell onto me, grabbing my throat. His momentum carried both of us to the ground. The force of his body weight being thrown against me held me there, beneath him. He couldn't fight, for he threw no punches, however his weight and the violent threshing motion, with his hands pressurising my throat, was becoming overwhelming. I called out, only managing a stifled cry above his animalistic groans.

A white coated arm grabbed him by the shoulder and then another white coated man dragged him to his feet. They led him away, as I tried not to cough and splutter too much, hoping to make light of the incident which I'd inflamed.

I sat there on the grass, watching the two male nurses drag Xebec inside. Babette stared back at me from the painting, the look in her eyes unfathomable. She seemed to wonder, *What have you done to my brother?*

"Dougay, are you alright?" called Ljuba, running from the building. I held up my hand to indicate that I was. She took hold of it and helped me to my feet. I brushed myself down and all the while Babette continued to stare.

"Do you wish to make a complaint?" Ljuba asked.

"No, no, no. I'll be okay." I'd caused enough trouble this Christmas morning.

"What did you say to him?" she asked.

I picked grass from my new scarf. "I only said that the Madonna was very beautiful."

I had lied to Ljuba, though I hadn't lied to Babette.

Xebec's portrait captured her beauty, perhaps a little too well, giving it an aura, a beauty beyond reality, an idealised and idolised love. I wondered if every destroyed canvas of her, with the punched in face, had been completed to this artistic level. Of course they had been.

Xebec was imprisoned in an artistic cycle. Beginning with passion and desire, he'd paint Babette's face and over time her eyes would stare back at him, until under the weight of all her accusations and his mounting guilt, when he'd finally completed the painting of the baby, he would snap, lashing out. He had hit her to rid his torment, though I reckoned he had always been hitting out at himself.

As I followed Ljuba from the garden back to the building, I glanced back one last time at the unfinished portrait. Babette's piercing green eyes bore through me. This time they seemed to be begging, *forgive me.*

Chapter 18

I was back from the clinic in time to move some of the café's small tables together and to lay a single table cloth over them all. I set out knives and forks and wine glasses. I didn't know how many people to expect so I made as many settings as the table formation allowed. I don't know what Louise was doing in the kitchen for no matter what it was it sure smelt wonderful. In fact, it smelt better than last night, if that were remotely possible.

"Can you smell this, Claude?" I asked, making my point a little too heavily. "Someday soon, we could sell Louise's cooking on a Friday and Saturday night. It doesn't have to be a total commitment to hot food – just a special weekend treat – like a limited edition. Deny the public what they're desperately after, and they'll turn out for it."

"The public, Dougay, are not desperately wanting to eat here. There are hundreds of places in Nice – and all have a reputation long earned before you became a shareholder in *L'Opera Mozart*." He placed three flutes on the table and cracked a bottle of bubbly. "You only have five percent. I'd hate to think of what crazy ideas you'd come up with if you owned ten!"

I watched him carefully pour the glasses. "So early in the day, Claude? Are you sure you're not part Australian?" He glanced up not comprehending. "It's not yet noon."

He scoffed. "There is a difference. In France we drink a lot; in Australia you swallow a lot."

"Touché!" I laughed.

Claude called out, "Louise! I have a glass for you."

Louise came out from the kitchen, wiping her hands on her full-length apron. Claude handed her the flute and we toasted each other. I gave them each a box of chocolates.

Louise sat and became teary. "I have nothing for you," she admitted.

"Yes, you do, you have a wonderful smile, and an ability to cook a superb meal."

"Why are you so good to me, Dougay?" she asked honestly. "Should I be suspicious?"

"No, no, no, Louise – not Dougay," said Claude. "He wears his heart on his sleeve and he is an open book."

"I think you've mixed your metaphors there, Claude," I smiled.

"Besides," continued Claude ignoring me, "he is in love with my solicitor."

I looked at Claude. How'd he know that? "No, I'm not. She's going to marry the Mayor."

Claude sat back a little. "I hadn't heard. I'm sorry, Mon Ami."

He patted me on the knee. If he hadn't, I'd have gone on believing that Francine's engagement to the Mayor was no big deal. From the moment I felt Claude's caring touch and saw the sympathetic look in his eyes, I knew how I truly felt about

Francine's engagement. There is nothing like Christmas to facilitate a wound to the heart.

Claude turned to Louise. "Never fear anything from Dougay – except his crazy ideas. Now, let's have another." He gathered the three flutes and refilled them.

My mobile rang. It was Mary-Anne.

"Are you in Cannes?" I asked hopefully.

"No, New York!"

"Oh."

Mary-Anne sensed the disappointment in my voice. "It's very early here. Merry Christmas, Dougay!"

What can you say of importance to someone, in a short period of time, overheard by two well-meaning though very inquisitive co-workers? Not much. And that's what I said.

"Merry Christmas, Dougay." Mary-Anne hung up.

On the dot of midday, Remy arrived with a jeroboam of bubbly and an enormous box of liquor chocolates under his arm. "Ho! Ho! Ho!" he sung loudly as he pushed open the café's front door. "This is a gift from a friend of a friend. He works as a travelling salesman for a confectionary distributor."

"No Angelie?" I asked, looking behind him.

"She'll try and drop by later."

Jules St Croix happily danced, exaggeratedly, through the door. He had with him a cake. Around his neck was his camera. I took the cake from him, thanked him, and immediately had my photograph taken. "Who's the beautiful waitress?" he asked.

"Chef – she's more than a waitress. Her name is Louise and she's my protégé. When you taste her cooking, tell Claude how wonderful it is. I have big plans for the café which involve her." Jules went off to take her picture.

I was pleased Audric came. He entered silently waving and placed two bottles of quality red wine onto the table. I introduced him to Remy, explaining to Audric that he was the dodgy man with the second-hand furniture business.

"Dodgy?" queried Remy, in mock offence. I left them to discuss the possibility of emptying Audric's house. I did not say that I saw Xebec this morning, and certainly did not say what happened to me and what I believed I had found out. I don't think I could ever say to Audric what I believed I had discovered.

The six of us sat around the table and raised our glasses. I was about to propose a toast to us all, when the door opened and a voice asked, "I'm not too late, am I?"

"Serge! Come on in!" shouted Remy. "Dougay, you remember Serge – looks after that block of apartments …"

"Yes, of course. Come on in, Serge. Take a seat. Claude – another glass, for Serge."

I remembered Serge. He was the caretaker, where in the basement of his building, unbeknownst to him, Calvin de Marko and Belinda Swann had performed their atrocities on Eloise and Danielle.

I remained standing at the head of the table and began again, "A toast! To all of us – the lonely guys and gal."

They chorused back to me, "The lonely guys and gal!"

Jules took a photo.

*

Everyone ate too much and everyone drank too much and I talked too much. I regaled them with stories of an exceedingly hot Christmas day on Bondi Beach, when people had to run and skip wildly to get across the boiling hot sand and into the freezing cold water. Remy doubted that. Jules said we Australians should move Christmas to winter. I said, "Australians have – 'Christmas in July', they call it! Only in the Southern Hemisphere do we have two Christmases!"

Louise began to collect the plates and cutlery. Claude said, "No. You cooked. We will wash up. Well, Dougay can, as he is the most experienced here at doing so." Everyone laughed. Not even on Christmas day were my friends going to let an opportunity go by.

Later in the afternoon, Audric bid 'adieu' and thanked everyone profusely. I think he had enjoyed being with us. It was certainly different to any of the other forty Christmas days he'd somehow managed to survive.

Around four in the afternoon, three people walked into the café. Jules saw them first, "Holy shit," he muttered. I looked up to see Madame Legrande on the arms of her two sons, Pierre and Raphael. Jules lent into me. "It's true! You do know the Brothers Legrande. I do not know whether to become your best friend, or never speak to you again."

I stood and welcomed them. Claude handed them each a glass of bubbly. Madame did not refuse. "My favourite," she said, "because Dougay is paying for it!" People laughed!

"So," said Pierre, looking about, "this is the investment one hears so much about. In years to come, people will say that it was here that Dougay Roberre first stepped forth on his path to great wealth."

Remy grabbed me by the arm and led me to the front door where Angelie was standing, taking off her coat. She'd come. Remy was pleased and so was I. She was with someone – and when her face turned to me and smiled in recognition, I couldn't hold back my joy. "Eloise!" We hugged like long lost friends.

She showed no signs of the trauma brought on by the bruises and scratch marks inflicted upon her by that deceased Hollywood asshole, and his equally famous and sadistic spouse. Her smile was radiant, her green eyes sparkling. Time heals, as the cliché goes.

M'sieur Pom knocked politely before entering. No one heard him. Louise noticed him and tugged at my arm. I called to him, "M'sieur Pom!" He stood aside and ushered in his wife. "Madame Pom!"

"The elusive saviour from up on the top floor," said Madame Pom, taking off her coat, "who looks over all us mere mortals below."

Between her and Madame Legrande, French women of a certain age sure have a way with words.

The gathering bubbled along until there came a cry from the front door and Milovic stood there with his family and Milos from *Vlatava-Elbe*. "Make way!" he shouted. "We have brought slivovitz!"

My first Christmas gathering in Nice was a roaring success!

*

"What's the matter, Louise?" I asked, pulling out a chair and sitting opposite her. Everyone had gone home, Claude had climbed his stairs to bed, and we were the only two left to clean and lock up. "You look concerned about something – post party blues?"

"It's late. The hostel will be closed."

I thought about that and all its ramifications. Even if she could somehow manage to get in, I didn't want her walking there at this time of night.

"Come on. Come home with me. I have a sofa and I'll even give you my pink duvet – the one Princess Grace bequeathed me."

"Who?"

Yes, of course, young people may never have heard of her. I was starting to feel I was definitely on the downhill side of forty.

She hesitated. I understood her reticence. "What guarantees can I give you that I'll keep my hands to myself?" I answered my own question. "None. Anyway, you're not my type – you're not aged and infirm and blind, deaf and dumb. And," I paused, "you're not rich!"

Everyone in my apartment block was asleep. We didn't take the elevator, rather tip-toed up the six flights. I pointed to the sofa, which wasn't difficult as there wasn't much else in the room to point to. I showed her my newly renovated bathroom. Louise was impressed. After visiting it, she sat on the sofa and I handed her my duvet.

"You sleep under this?" she asked. I said I did. "Then I feel very safe here tonight." She laughed.

I turned out the lights and with two pairs of socks on my feet I stretched out under my one blanket and the new overcoat that Francine had bought me in Milan.

Christmas day was over and the streets outside offered no sound of movement, as the apartments on all the floors below us had done. It was as if the entire population of Nice had decided they'd had enough of Christmas Day. I'd drunk a lot and was pleased I had spaced it out over time, as I'm sure if I hadn't, my bedroom now would be spinning.

Louise raised her voice, projecting it across the living room and through my open bedroom door.

"Do you love your mother, Dougay?"

It was a strange question. I wondered if I'd understood it correctly. "Yes – very much so. Though unfortunately, she's dead."

"Oh." There was silence.

"You?" I asked. "From the question I get the feeling you don't."

She didn't reply. I turned onto my side and gathered the overcoat around my ears.

"You once asked me if I wanted to be an actress." She had my attention now. I rolled onto my back and listened.

"I thought I did. My mother took me to an audition. I thought I recognised that woman – the one who owned the suitcase I ran off with. I did recognise her – eventually. She was at the audition."

I didn't say anything, waiting for Louise to continue.

"She didn't remember me. Why should she? I was just a fourteen-year-old girl being dragged along by an ambitious mother."

Silence returned. I closed my eyes, thinking the conversation was over, that all Louise wanted to do was make the connection for me between her and Mary-Anne.

"It was on a boat – the audition – upstairs. I had to sing a little, and dance a little, and read from a script. All the while my mother flirted with the fat American producer. Yes, that woman would never remember me. She was only downstairs welcoming the other girls and their mothers. *Helga*. I think the film was called. *Helga* – about a German girl."

"*Heidi* – and I think she's Swiss." I'd remembered what Mary-Anne had told me. "How long ago was this?"

"I was fourteen – five years ago. The film never happened. That bastard never delivered on his promise."

I wondered how far I could ease her thoughts forward, for I hoped the truth wasn't going to be too painful. "You had the part?" I asked innocently. "You'd been cast as Heidi?"

"Mother believed I had. I believed I had."

"It must have been a good audition you gave."

"I wasn't promised the role because of the audition."

I started to get that sinking feeling in my stomach. What I'd learnt about Harold Kempenski over the past few months, prepared me for the worst of what Louise may begin to say. I waited for her to go on.

Eventually Louise asked, "Are you still awake?"

"Yes."

The apartment returned to silence, until she gathered her thoughts, or rather her approach to wording them once again.

"After I'd been told I'd won the role, the very next night, my mother dragged me to a hotel in Cannes. She was going to reward the producer for me being cast. She insisted all I had to do was just kiss him – with my clothes off – while she did it."

I imagined Kempenski living out his fantasy and shuddered. Then I said, trying to console her, "Perhaps she was protecting you."

"Protecting me?"

"Yes. She screwed Kempenski, so he'd keep his hands off you."

"She whored herself and dragged me along!" Louise was having none of my suggestion.

"How did this come about?" she asked rhetorically. "What parent can do that to their child? My mother was, and still is, an amateur whore – the worst kind. She fucked him while I kissed him and whispered in his ear, the lines I'd memorised from the script, delivered in my best 'Heidi' voice. That's what he wanted. That's what I had to do to seal the deal."

Again, there was silence. How many questions could I ask before appearing to be too inquisitive?

"Louise," I started, "you said a hotel."

"Yes – in Cannes."

"Not a basement – in Nice?"

Again silence. It now felt colder than before.

Louise said in a very serious tone, "Why do you not believe me, Dougay?"

"Oh, I do. Believe me, Louise, I certainly do."

I lay there, eyes on the dark ceiling. I said, hesitatingly, "Louise – I wish to ask you something – a little blunt – a little straightforward – a 'yes' or 'no' answer will suffice."

"Okay," she agreed.

"Did the producer sexually penetrate you at all?"

"No."

She *had* been protected by her mother. The woman had sensed the type of man Kempenski was – he'd probably propositioned her for a threesome with her daughter. The older woman knew that once she'd drained the mogul, his desire for her daughter would evaporate.

"I never got the part and after a year I left my mother and have been living – well, you can guess."

*

I would like to say that after Christmas my life returned to a quieter pace. It didn't. New Year's Eve was spent at *Vlatava-Elbe*.

I drank slivovitz. I danced with Ulna. I drank beer. I laughed with Milovic. I drank slivovitz. I danced with Ljuba. I laughed with Pasha. I ate oblozene chlebicky. I danced with Ulna a second time. I drank beer. By mistake I kissed Remy goodnight!!!

Once again after midnight, I instinctively found my way to the sea. However, I didn't jump in this time to sober up. It was far too cold, and in my state of inebriation, I may never have climbed back out. I stood holding onto a bench, gulping in huge mouthfuls of sea breeze. With my mouth so wide, I feared a sea gull might shit in it from above. There were none about – it was either too cold for them, or they'd been invited to a party elsewhere.

I remembered that it was on such a night as this I'd wandered off to Francine's and was rebuffed. I wished Mary-Anne was here – to hold me; to keep me warm; to listen to my dreams, my hopes, and my desires. I hate being drunk. I can kind of accept the hangover and the feeling of death it brings on me, though I can never forgive myself for becoming so sentimental and maudlin.

I must have fallen asleep and luckily wasn't woken by a patrolling policeman. Maybe they were all off quelling more outrageous forms of celebratory drunkenness. It was nearly 6am when I opened my eyes. I stumbled off on the long walk home. Several minutes later at precisely 6am my mobile rang.

"Happy New Year!" shouted a tipsy Mary-Anne above background cheering. "I'm in Times Square!"

Chapter 19

A week later, Audric phoned me. "Dougay, can I ask a very big favour of you, please?"

"Sure, Audric, anything. What is it?"

"Could you accompany me today, please? I have to go to the morgue and identify Xebec."

I sat upright and managed to force out, "What?"

As Audric repeated what he'd said, I thought of the incident with Xebec, his explosive temper, his violence, my touching of the raw nerve when I asked him about having had sex with his sister. I hoped to high heaven I had not in any way brought about his suicide.

"How?" I asked. "How did it happen? How did he die?"

"A heart attack." I breathed a lot easier. "He'd been growing more violent. He destroyed that painting he was working on before completion. He'd begun wrestling with the nurses. During a struggle with them, he managed to flee down the upstairs corridor. He had a violent seizure and collapsed at the top of the staircase. He fell and hit his head several times on the long flight down."

*

Three days later I went with Audric to the funeral. On the way there I relived over and over the violent Christmas day incident and my provocation of Xebec. Since my arrival in Nice, I had accumulated secrets – secrets I'm not going to reveal to anyone – and that meeting with Xebec would be the one I'd not tell Audric. I admonished myself, for even though Xebec had died of a heart attack, I felt that I had obliquely contributed to it.

Xebec was cremated and his ashes placed into a slot in a wall. Only Audric and I stood before it. I hoped when I finally kicked off this mortal coil there'd be a few more than two waving farewell. After the funeral, we went back to Audric's place. He brewed his excellent coffee.

Handing me a mug, he said, "Thank you for the invitation to your Christmas lunch. I had a wonderful time, sitting back, listening to the stories of others. Being around happily carousing people was an experience I now realize I'd thoroughly missed. You're a generous man, Dougay. These days there is a dwindling supply of generosity. People think only of themselves. I wish you well with your five percent investment."

"Thank you, Audric."

We toasted each other with coffee.

Audric looked about his living room, taking it all in. "There's no longer anything to keep me here. Call your friend Remy. Ask him to come and value my furniture."

*

Remy came and went through Audric's house, noting down every item, assessing what value the furniture had and what profit margin he'd have in taking it. I told Remy that Audric expected all of it to go, that once he left he wanted to leave it all behind. I knew Audric was planning on only taking memories, not keepsakes.

Remy quoted Audric a price and he accepted. "Audric," said Remy, "call me when you have a sale for your place and you are ready to leave. We can get everything out in a day."

They shook hands. Remy and I headed out.

"Please, wait a moment," Audric said. We stopped by the doorway. Audric went inside and returned a little later with an old battered suitcase. He did not carry it by the handle rather he cradled it in his arms. In balanced hands he extended it towards me. "Dougay, I'd appreciate it, if you could burn this, please. I trust you to take care of it. Baby clothes – you understand?"

I nodded. Audric passed it to me, carefully, as if bestowing it upon me.

Remy drove me home to Avenue Auber. As he parked out front, half wedged on the footpath, he said, "I have a small wood burner. I can get rid of that for you."

"No, Remy. Audric entrusted that to me. It's the least I can do."

"Where are you going to burn it?" he asked, knowing my apartment did not have an open fireplace.

"I'll probably bring it back to you. However, for now, I just want to…I feel I owe him…"

"You're an odd person, Dougay."

I smiled. "Coming from you, Remy, I'll take that as a compliment."

I climbed down and he drove off. I took the suitcase upstairs.

I stretched back on my lounge and thought of what I'd learnt about Audric. I now knew he was the jeweller, Carvell Lefbvre, the one Raphael had spoken of, though Audric had never spoken of being a jeweller to me.

I knew his baby went missing. If it was a kidnapping, then why didn't Audric ever say anything to the police? As a jeweller he'd have been a target for unscrupulous people as he'd have been regarded as being rich and vulnerable. If a ransom was paid, then why wasn't the child returned? If it was a bungled exchange, then afterwards, why did Audric and Babette only report the baby as missing? Or was that 'missing' conclusion brought by Raphael's old detective friend? However, a baby doesn't go missing. That implies the baby doesn't wish to be found and no baby is capable of that. I had no answer, though it didn't stop me wondering. Maybe the child was never taken for a ransom. Maybe the abductors already had a sale for the baby.

The one sure thing I felt, was that the reason Babette had changed so markedly during the marriage, was that her half-brother Xebec had raped her. It had to have been something as traumatic as that to bring on such a sudden change in her personality. And of course, Babette never told her husband.

I knew Xebec had an obsession with his half-sister. He'd paint her face so perfectly detailed and realized, it was an image for him to worship. Then her bright green eyes would work their way into his warped thinking and he'd snap in a moment of lucidity and self-awareness. Ljuba had told me, he never hit the face of the child, only the face of the Madonna – Babette.

I recalled again Audric's early statement to me. Yes, his heart had been slowly broken, though Babette wasn't gaining inner strength. He'd misread that. Babette was withdrawing from reality.

Was the baby the product of that incestuous union? Did Xebec take the baby? Did he know the child was his and therefore claimed it? If so, what did he do with it? I felt again the strength of his rage on Christmas morning and I hoped he'd not killed the boy. If he had taken him, I hoped he'd passed off the child to a loving couple who raised him. I hoped baby Donadieu was not given to God, rather that he went on to live a life – a life as fortunate as mine. We'd both be the same age now.

How ironic that Audric financially supported Xebec in his years of hospitalization – never realising that he'd raped his wife and fathered his only child.

I lifted the suitcase onto the table. I did – and didn't – wish to open it. I'm wary about opening up time capsules. The past belongs where it is, however Audric had wanted me to take care of this suitcase. He wanted me to treat these possessions with dignity. I opened the lid.

There was a flattened rag doll, roughly sewn, homemade, the little blue sailor shorts faded through time, though still neatly pressed as the day they were put on the doll and packed away. There was a matching pair, a little larger for the baby boy to wear, packed neatly below a matching sailor top. Below that there were several baby blankets and tops and shorts and little socks and baby shoes and booties. I picked up a bell on a rattle. It still rang clear. I was delving into the tragedy of a family I felt I'd come to know, though of course, never did. I saw Babette making these clothes, packing them away with tears in her beautiful green eyes knowing that baby

Donadieu was never coming home. I saw Audric trying to reach his wife and she shutting him out.

I came across a letter addressed simply, 'Audric.'

I stopped searching through the suitcase. The clothing I'd removed remained neatly stacked by the suitcase on my table.

I pinned the letter on my message board in the exact place I had pinned the photographs of Danielle and the fifty euro note Eloise had left me.

I went back to the suitcase.

The remaining clothing I stacked on the existing pile. Freed of its belongings the bag released its mustiness. It smelled old.

Beneath my kitchen sink, I found a cloth and wiped inside the suitcase. Why would I do that when I knew I was burning it? I felt I owed it to Audric to at least clean it. As I wiped the base, the old material covering came away.

There was a small black cloth pouch inside. I opened its drawstring. I emptied the contents into my palm. Ten cut diamonds sparkled back at me.

Chapter 20

I knocked on the metal door of Remy's warehouse and waited. I knocked again. The single steel door opened and Remy peered around suspiciously.

"Oh, it's only you. What are you doing here so soon?" He glanced down at the small suitcase I was carrying. "The burner is out the back."

I walked in by him, ignoring his offer. He locked the door behind me. I turned and asked, "Do you read French?"

"What a stupid question! Of course, I read French."

"Good – because I don't."

"What?"

"I read English!" I crossed to his desk and carefully placed the suitcase of baby's clothing on the floor beside it.

Remy, sensing that there was something bothering me, asked concerned, "What is it?"

"I don't know. I need your help. Before you read this," I took the letter out of my goatskin jacket, "I need to swear you to secrecy."

"Why secrecy, if you…"

"Please, Remy. Swear!" I surprised myself – I'd never been short tempered with him before.

"Okay, okay, I swear."

"Sit at your desk," I suggested. "I'll lean over you."

He did and cleared a space on it. I handed him the letter. He looked at the envelope. "Audric," he read aloud.

"I can read *that*!"

Remy laughed. I snorted a release and patted him on his shoulder. I hadn't realized how tense I'd become walking over here.

"Can you point to the words as we go along, please?"

"Okay." Remy took the letter out from its envelope and began to read.

My dearest darling Audric – I have always loved you. You are not to blame, I am. Forgive me.

It was love at first sight – the day I was employed by your father – and I saw you there. The day we married, I was never happier.

Remy looked up at me. "Why do you hold such importance for a love letter?"

"Read on."

From the time I was a teenager, Xebec had always stared at me. He took too much interest in me. He tried to watch me undress. He tried to watch me in the shower. He'd wait for me after school and walk me home, trying to hold my hand. He wanted to own me.

Remy stopped reading. "Who's Xebec?"

"Audric's half brother-in-law. Read on."

When you and I married, he grew worse. He no longer restrained his feelings. He'd come to our place and stand in the corner – remember? His eyes followed me everywhere. Then three months after our wedding he snapped. I was raped by him. I knew his seed was growing inside me and not your seed. I had been impregnated by the devil. He had come to me in the disguise of my half-brother.

Remy stopped again and put down the letter, gathering his breath. He was becoming as unsettled as I was. He cleared his throat and continued.

I should have got rid of the foetus, but I could not disobey God's law. How could such a devoted child of God, as I am, do that?

I gave birth. The nurse passed me the child. I handed it on to you. I let you believe it was yours. Forgive me. It wasn't yours. Every time you held him, I knew he wasn't yours.

The child's eyes bore into me – accusing me. God was looking into my tarnished soul.

The child's cries flooded my ears – admonishing me. God was damning me.

I tried to shut out my unforgiving God. I covered my ears. I covered my eyes. No amount of hiding, burying my face in cushions could ever shut out God's accusations.

I told you God spoke to me and said I was to call our son 'Donadieu'. He presented me the solution in the child's name – 'Given to God'.

You were away for a night – a perfect opportunity – valuing a client's diamonds in Marseille. I took the child and cast it out. I cast out my sin – as God had always wanted me to do. The child lies cleansed in the Mediterranean.

I wrote the ransom note. I wouldn't let you see it, remember? In a fit of false emotion, I tossed it into the fire, remember? I fell and you caught me and while you held me there, I was buying time for the note to burn behind me. Water and fire. Am I ever to be washed clean of sin? Or am I to burn in hell for eternity?

You gathered the ransom in jewels and intended to deliver them. There was no one to deliver them to. That night I fed you laxatives in your meal, causing your sudden illness. I put you to bed, and for your eyes I took the ransom to the 'kidnappers'.

I lied to you that they stole the jewellery. I am a great sinner – but I am no thief. The jewellery never left the house.

Forgive me. Forgive me. Forgive me.

I can no longer live with myself.

Babette.

Chapter 21

I had no intention of showing Audric the letter. It didn't matter that it was intended for him, I couldn't do it. He didn't need to read such a devastating truth at his age.

I am not a thief, so the diamonds I wouldn't keep from him. However, I faced a dilemma. How was I going to explain their existence? And the fact that I'd found them in the suitcase of baby Donadieu's clothing?

I sat in Audric's living room, in front of the boarded-up fireplace, in which Babette had burned the 'ransom note'.

I handed him the small black pouch. He pulled apart the short draw strings, glancing up at me, not understanding. He emptied the contents into his hand. After a moment of recognition, he slumped back into his chair, his fingers folding around his palm, not letting the stones slip from his grasp.

"I told you Donadieu died," he began, weakly. "I apologise for lying to you." He returned the diamonds to their pouch and pulled tight the drawstring. "He was kidnapped. These are the jewels – the ransom. How did you find them?"

I was ready to tell him what I knew, what I supposed and what I was prepared to invent.

However, before I could, he said, "The night of the ransom exchange, I was suddenly taken ill. I couldn't go and deliver it. Babette took these to the kidnappers. She said they were handed over, but no child was given to her. The kidnappers ran off. She returned distraught. I said it was time to inform the police. 'An abduction! Not a kidnapping!' she begged me. She insisted. 'I've let you down! Forgive me!' she cried."

I leant forward and put my hand on his knee, trying to console him. He wasn't aware of my gesture.

"I told the police the baby had disappeared. We never hinted at a ransomed kidnapping. I suppose Babette wanted to protect her shame for losing our child. I don't really know. I just know that I agreed. I went along." He looked at me. "What man doesn't go along with what his wife, whom he loves deeply, wants?"

He stood and paced a little. "Do you know for how many years I glanced in prams, then carefully studied toddlers and then early school children? I stopped doing that once a school teacher warned me to move on."

After a time, I said, "Audric, I believe Babette took the jewels to hand over, but the kidnappers never turned up. Your baby was already gone – into the arms of some desperately loving couple. Babette returned here heartbroken, and hid the jewels from you in the baby's suitcase. Yes, as you say, feeling guilty at her failure to deliver her promise to you."

That was all I wanted to offer. I'd lied enough to Audric.

*

Raphael Legrande was not waiting for me on the footpath outside Le Grande Nice restaurant. I found him inside talking to his friend, the Maître d', accompanied by a beautiful woman on his arm. It was the doctor who'd X-rayed me. I'd dressed appropriately for my second meal at his wonderful restaurant. I had on my Milanese dark grey suit, the warm woollen overcoat and, perched on my head, the stylish fedora.

As I entered Raphael looked up. "Well, well. Last time he looked like an ordinary criminal. Now he looks like a corporate one."

"I hope you're paying," I replied. "I've left my corporate credit card at home."

He laughed and introduced me to Doctor Constance Armand. I thanked her for the X-ray.

Doctor Armand said, "Don't thank me. Thank our quick-thinking detective here, and his fine work in suppressing the escape of an international criminal."

The three of us were shown to our table. The food and wine was as superb as I remembered them to be. During dinner I told Raphael of what I knew about the Lefbvre baby. He was impressed. Doctor Armand was enthralled.

I glanced up to the entranceway and quickly looked away. The dapper gentleman from Aubagne walked in with three others. They were M. Baldy, M. Beret and Marcel who was wearing my scarf – the scarf Madame Legrande had knitted – the one which had been souvenired at that roadside dump near Aix-en-Provence.

Raphael, with his detective's eye, saw my quick reaction and asked quietly, "You know Monsieur Heroux?"

I did not reply.

"Louis Heroux is not a welcome guest in our city of Nice," Raphael went on, looking at Dr Armand though explaining for the both of us. "He's from the west. I fear he is wishing to make some splashes in the calm waters of our settled underworld."

"That asshole had me beaten up," I whispered.

Now my assault made sense to Raphael. "How did you manage to cross *him*?"

"It was nothing to do with his criminal activities – rather, I embarrassed and humiliated his recently acquired lover – the one with him, preening." I went on to explain about Marcel and his relationship with Claude.

"And," I added, "He's at this minute, hanging up on the coat rack, the lost scarf your mother knitted for me. I have to leave. I don't wish to be recognised. Is there a back way out of here?"

Raphael called over the Maître d' and whispered, explaining to him.

"Come, monsieur," the Maître d' said to me. I bid Raphael and Constance goodbye.

"Thanks for clearing that up," whispered the pleased detective. "The ghost of detective LaCrosse rests well tonight."

I ducked out through the kitchen. I stopped inside and said to the Maître d', "Monsieur, I'm sorry. But I've left my overcoat – and my hat!"

"One moment, Monsieur."

I waited amongst the familiar surroundings, though the kitchen at *L'Opera Mozart* was nowhere near as busy, nor as elaborately fitted out as this one. The Maître d' returned with my coat and hat. I thanked him, and he opened the fire exit for me.

Stepping into the alley behind, I shook myself into the overcoat, and as I always did when first putting it on, I thought of Francine's generosity. I placed the fedora carefully on my head, giving it just enough of a tilt, so as not to lose any of my rakishness.

Down the alley, in from the entrance to the street, were two dark, parked cars, one behind the other. The two drivers were sharing a cigarette in the night air. I've had experiences with parked cars, so I scuffed my feet and making a false stumble, staggered a few paces as if I'd drunk too much. I noticed the nearest car had an Italian rear number plate. As I passed the two suited men, I uttered slovenly, "Bon soir, mes amis!" As I turned back to wave to them, they returned my friendliness with a combined look of contempt. The first car had a French licence plate. I guessed only one was driving to Italy tonight.

*

After ten the next morning, Raphael called me. "I thought you'd like to know about the outcome of last night's meal."

"Go on," I said, "I'm all ears."

"They were celebrating something. They'd ordered champagne and toasted the one you call 'Marcel'. It seemed he's off on a holiday to Italy. I walked over to their table and showed them my badge. Then I asked to see some identification. They objected, until Heroux raised his hand, silencing his three goons. I warned the dapper gentleman that his terrain was much further to the west. He said he was only eating here because he was a personal friend of the owner. I didn't tell him I was half of the owner. I phoned my brother this morning, and he said he despises Heroux."

"So, I looked at Marcel's ID. I asked him if he was the gentleman who once worked for Claude at café *L'Opera Mozart*. He reluctantly said he was. I told him I had a message for him from Claude."

Raphael paused. I waited.

"I said to him: Claude asked me to tell you, if I ever bumped into you, that his tests have come back positive."

I laughed.

"That bastard Heroux's face fell to the floor. I don't think he and Marcel have been practising safe sex!"

*

Two mornings later, I woke and turned on the television news. I'd been getting into that habit over the past few days. I'd also been bringing home, after work the previous evening, a stale croissant. After lathering it in blackberry conserve, I'd swallow it with the aid of my freshly brewed black coffee. I was enjoying my new morning habit, as I was beginning to match some of the words sliding across the lower screen with what the presenter was saying.

A close-up image of a crashed fuselage caught my eye. The accompanying title read something like, 'Light Plane Crash near Marseille'. I listened as the presenter went on to explain.

The plane had been flying too low and the pre-dawn fog had made visibility impossible. The voiceover said the reason that it was flying low was to avoid radar detection.

Then across the bottom of the screen flashed: 'Cocaine Plane! 500kgs splattered on Galaban Mountain'.

I recognized that place. It was the mountain outside Aubagne.

There were images of the cocaine in bags, the majority of them sealed, however some had been busted open on impact. I cynically wondered how many day trippers would be heading up there in a day or two with their heads imitating tracker dogs.

Across the screen it read, "Calabrian Mafia ..." I couldn't catch the remainder, the words slid by too quickly.

Rescue workers and ambulance men were lifting two stretchered bodies from the wreckage. The second body, after being lifted, was returned to the ground. The ambulance man tucked something in under, or he adjusted the sheet covering around the corpse, as I couldn't quite tell. They lifted the stretcher and walked out of screen. I'd hate to be an ambulance man.

I felt a shiver shoot up me, though the image had been and gone. I hoped it was on another television station. Picking up the remote, I channel surfed, finding the same news item. I watched intensely. Yes, something had slipped out of the stretcher, and had been lifted up under the corpse's sheet. It was the first scarf Madame Legrande had knitted me.

Chapter 22

Louise was doing longer shifts at the café, so I had a little spare time on my hands. I was happy she was and she was happy with the work – happy to have money in her pocket and not need to go running off into the night with someone's suitcase so she could eat.

In the days after Marcel's tragic demise, I thought of that parked car with the Italian license plate; of his relationship with the criminal Heroux; the cocaine in the crashed plane; the sachet of cocaine up my ass; and how Marcel's association had ironically brought about his demise. I hoped the short-lived affair with his new motorbike had been worthwhile. If he'd stayed with Claude, he'd still be alive. I knew above all, I wasn't going to tell Claude what I'd put together.

I phoned Raphael and asked if they'd identified the passenger in the crashed plane. He told me it wasn't his case, however he felt sure they hadn't. I reminded him of the joke he played on Marcel and Heroux. I reminded him how Marcel appeared to be going away to Italy. I reminded him of Marcel hanging his mother's scarf on the coat rack in his restaurant. I told him to tell the investigating detectives to have a closer look at the television footage of the crash site and at the clothes of their corpse in the morgue.

When there was a morsel of winter sun, I sat in Place Mozart with or without Madame Legrande. With her, I'd let her reminisce of a life well spent. Without her, I'd dream of Mary-Anne and what she may be working on.

I longed for the winter to be gone and late spring to be here, for Mary-Anne had promised to return in the summer. We could once again take *The Blue Dahlia* to the Italian beach and let the warmth of the sun and the cool of the water enhance our enjoyment of each other.

I had plans for *L'Opera Mozart*. Xebec's paintings had got me thinking, though I hadn't really formulated a solid idea and Claude would never go for anything half baked. I could wait. I had the rest of winter to get my thoughts together.

Audric found a buyer for his place and Remy and I cleaned it out. "My fee for helping you Remy, is the unused bed from Audric's second bedroom. I need a bed for mine." Remy grumbled, however, of course, he acquiesced.

We carried it in through the foyer and naturally M'sieur Pom complained, though he still managed to hold open the iron doors of the elevator for us.

The next day I stood with Audric inside Gare de Nice in front of the ticket barriers. He had a large suitcase with him. Remy had in storage his other clothes, to be forwarded, once he'd found a place in Paris he wished to call home.

"Thank you for everything, Dougay," said Audric, with his hand placed gently on my arm. "I didn't think a person at my age could acquire a new friend."

"It's never too late." I shook his hand. "It's been a pleasure, Audric. I'll miss our walks." He bent and unzipped the outer section of the suitcase. He reached inside. "Audric, you still have a lot to offer, remember that."

"In regard to what?" he asked, genuinely interested.

"A woman – a happy coda to your life."

"A woman? At my age?"

"Yes, you have honesty; a sense of responsibility; and you're simply a nice guy. A lot of women crave that in a partner."

"Perhaps," he shrugged. "You should consider buying a larger share in your café," he added enigmatically.

He handed me a large envelope. "This is a small thank you. There is a certificate of authenticity; a bill of sale in our names; and a receipt. Everything is perfectly legitimate. I cannot take them with me, you understand – too many painful memories."

He squeezed my fingers around the documents. He paid particular attention in having me feel the pouch containing the ten diamonds. We embraced and he left me, walking through to the platform.

Stunned, looking after him, tears came to my eyes. Gripping the diamond pouch tightly, I called out loudly, hoping he'd hear, *"A bientot, Mate!"*